"Tristan is the closest thing I have to a brother. He's worried about you, and so am I. Let me help."

Fear flickered through Ashley's eyes as she whispered, "Someone almost ran me over."

"Tristan said something about a letter," Matt pressed.

Ashley nodded. "When I got home that day, there was an anonymous note saying that someone wanted his property back."

His gut clenched. What kind of jerk threatened a battered women's shelter? "Listen, I'm in town for a few days. Let me look into things."

She smiled up at him. "Thanks, but I got the note more than a week ago. If there was any danger, something else would have happened by now."

As they reached her car, her smile died. He didn't have to ask if she still thought the threat had passed as she took in the smashed windshield of her coupe. Tucked under a wiper blade, the person responsible for the mess had left a clear message.

If I don't get what's mine, you'll get what's yours.

Books by Liz Johnson

Love Inspired Suspense

The Kidnapping of Kenzie Thorn
Vanishing Act
Code of Justice
A Promise to Protect

LIZ JOHNSON

After graduating from Northern Arizona University in Flagstaff with a degree in public relations, Liz Johnson set out to work in the Christian publishing industry, which was her lifelong dream. In 2006 she got her wish when she accepted a publicity position with a major trade book publisher. While working as a publicist in the industry, she decided to pursue her other dream—becoming an author. Along the way to having her novels published, she wrote articles for several magazines and worked as a freelance editorial consultant.

Liz makes her home in Nashville, Tennessee, where she enjoys theater, exploring her new home and making frequent trips to Arizona to dote on her nephew and three nieces. She loves stories of true love with happy endings.

A PROMISE TO PROTECT

Liz Johnson

Recycling programs for this product may not exist in your area.

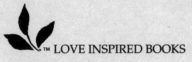 ™ LOVE INSPIRED BOOKS

ISBN-13: 978-0-373-44518-9

A PROMISE TO PROTECT

www.LoveInspiredBooks.com

Printed in U.S.A.

But he said to me, My grace is sufficient for you, for my power is made perfect in weakness. Therefore I will boast all the more gladly about my weaknesses, so that Christ's power may rest on me.

—2 Corinthians 12:9

For my Savior, who shows off His strength
through my weaknesses.

For my brother Micah,
who has been my champion and friend,
and my brother-in-law John,
who loves my sister like no one else could.
Thanks for being part of my family.

And for the men and women
who have served in the Armed Forces to
protect those who can't protect themselves,
including my dad and late grandpa, Clarence Dirks.

ONE

"When do you go wheels up?" Ashley Sawyer asked as she walked down the street toward the local grocery store several blocks away.

"I'm impressed," her brother teased, the warm amusement in his voice coming clearly through the phone line. "You've been paying attention to the lingo."

"And you're avoiding the question." Tristan had been deploying with his team of U.S. Navy SEALs since she was sixteen. She knew that when he didn't answer a question, it was usually because he *couldn't*. Stepping onto the curb, she asked, "Well, you and Matt just take care of each other, okay?"

Silence hung on the line for so long that she checked her phone to make sure she hadn't dropped the call. "Tristan?"

"Matt's not going this time."

Her heart squeezed just a bit. She'd counted on Matt Waterstone, her brother's best friend since their first day in SEAL training, to watch out for Tristan. Matt had a habit of being in the right place at the right time, protecting Tristan from at least one bullet during their deployments. And that was just what he would actually own up to.

She swallowed an unexpected lump in her throat at the

thought of harm coming to the man she'd had a crush on once upon a time. "What happened?"

"Nothing major. He'll heal up just fine with a little time. Hey, maybe I'll send him your way for a visit—keep him from getting bored here on his own."

Ashley chuckled as she stepped down from the curb to cross the street. "Right, I'm sure he'd have more fun in tiny little Charity Way, California, than in San Diego. Besides, I wouldn't have much time to entertain him. We just got a new guest at Lil's Place who needs somewhere to stay out of town. My next few days will be pretty full setting that up." Lil's Place had been housing battered women and their children for nearly ten years, and Ashley had served there for the past three. Within the past year she'd taken over as director of operations for the shelter. The new girl was her responsibility—along with all the other women and children at the shelter.

"Oh, Tristan, she's so young—maybe not even quite eighteen, and so petite. This guy must have been a monster, because she's bruised from her wrists all the way up to her elbows."

Her stomach swooped at just the thought of Joy, the young girl who had been dropped off the night before. If she had to guess, she'd say the girl was probably Korean, but Joy hadn't spoken more than a few words since arriving at Lil's, barely offering her name.

That was certainly understandable. It was hard to talk with anyone—let alone a stranger—after suffering at an abuser's hands. After all, Ashley hadn't spoken to anyone about it for months after the first time Paul hit her. Just the memory made her cheek sting, and she rubbed it absently as she entered the grocery store.

"Where'd she come from?" Tristan was always so straightforward. His question brought a wry grin to her lips.

Looking over her shoulder and around the end of the aisle to make sure she wouldn't be overheard in the store, Ashley whispered, "My friend Miranda dropped her off last night. She just said the girl needs to get out of town and asked if I knew of a place where she'd be safe."

A full-body shiver made her wrap her arms around her middle. She didn't like moving abuse victims out of Charity Way—leaving an abuser was traumatic enough without having to adjust to a new town—but in certain high-risk situations, it was necessary. Some abusive men went after their victims. Hadn't Paul come after her every time she broke things off? Every time she changed her phone number?

And Joy deserved to have a safe place to recover until she was ready to face her attacker.

Tristan let out a slow breath. "She's lucky to have you looking out for her. But don't forget to look out for yourself. You know what my rule number two is, right?"

"Don't fall out of the boat?"

He snorted. "Know your enemy. You've got to know who's been hurting this girl if your friend thinks there's a chance he'll come after her."

"And is rule number one as useful in this situation?"

"Don't get shot."

"All right. I won't. You don't either."

Having paid for a box of bandages and a compression wrap, Ashley exited the shop and started heading back home. As she crossed Main Street, she happened to glance to the side, directly into the reflection of the sun off of the windshield of a white sedan.

Suddenly its tires squealed against the pavement as the car barreled toward her, gaining speed with every inch.

Her mind froze, and her instincts took over as she fell

backward. Her hip slammed into the sidewalk just as the car flew by and disappeared down another side street.

All her breath gone, she sat on the ground, part of her hoping that someone else had seen the car and maybe gotten a license plate number, the other part of her hoping that no one had witnessed her graceless fall. Gulping in as much air as possible, she lifted a scraped palm and studied it with a strange detachment. It didn't hurt.

Yet.

Her brother's voice rang out clearly, and Ashley snatched the phone that she'd dropped, the motion sending fire through her wrist. She brushed her jacket sleeves out of the way to get a better look at the scraped skin.

"Ash, answer me! Are you okay?" Tristan sounded worried, as if he'd called her name several times.

Ashley closed her eyes against the morning sun and the throbbing at her temples. "I think someone just tried to run me over." The absurdity of the thought brought a laugh bubbling from deep inside. That was ridiculous. The driver must not have noticed her. "What am I saying? Some driver just wasn't paying attention and nearly hit me."

"Are you okay?"

"Yes." She glanced around for the car as she pushed herself to her feet. It was long gone and the whole thing clearly a mistake. Right?

Another voice echoed behind Tristan's, and the phone crackled a few times as if he'd covered the receiver with his hand. "Listen, I have to go in a minute, but I love you. And I don't tell you this enough, but I'm really proud of you, kid. Be careful, okay?"

"I will."

Ashley ended the call and slipped the phone into her pocket. With the bag in her hand swinging at her side, Ashley hurried back to Lil's Place, so intent on finalizing the arrangements to move Joy to a long-term house several counties away that she nearly forgot to check the mailbox as she strolled up the driveway.

Leaning back, she slipped her hand into the mailbox, pulling out only one envelope. After flipping it over, she frowned. Both sides were blank. But the generic card inside contained more than enough to send her stomach through the cement and make her wonder if the near hit-and-run earlier had been more than an accident.

Just because I missed you today, doesn't mean you can keep my property.

Matt Waterstone lowered himself from his truck, landing on his good leg and resting the injured one without a wince as he glanced up and down Main Street of Charity Way. As nice as the town looked, it wasn't where he wanted to be. The rest of his team had gone wheels up on an op that he hadn't even been briefed about. Tristan, Will and Zach had laughed about the fun they'd have without the senior chief, like he was a stick-in-the-mud.

Man, he wished he was going with them.

But at least he might be useful here, despite his doctor's orders to stay in San Diego, his leg propped up on a pillow. Tristan had a gut feeling that Ashley was in trouble, and after that gut feeling had saved them both from a sniper a year before, who was Matt to argue? After almost ten years with SEAL Team FIFTEEN, he'd learned to rely on his training and instinct. And he trusted Tristan's gut more than his own.

The details were still a bit slim at this point—a near hit-and-run and a note from some deranged creep. Apparently Tristan had been on the phone with Ashley during the hit-and-run, and Mrs. Sawyer had called Tristan after

Ashley told her about the note. It was enough to get Matt headed north.

"Just make sure that she's okay." Tristan had said, "Ash gets all kinds of calls and letters and snide remarks thanks to her work at the shelter. But no one's ever tried to run her over before. Just watch her back until they find this creep. Will you?"

Of course the answer was yes. His best friend's family was the closest thing Matt had to a family of his own.

"Excuse me." He approached a white-haired man writing the specials on a sidewalk chalkboard. "Could you point me in the direction of Lil's Place?" The man eyed him, as though questioning what business he could have there. "I'm a friend of Ashley Sawyer's."

Suddenly a small black coupe zipped down Main Street, screeching to a halt twenty yards to his right. Two women burst from within as if fireworks had been set off inside the car. They left the doors open; the petite blonde behind the wheel flew around the front of the car and hugged the other, a taller woman with dark hair.

"You'll be great, Carmen!" the blonde said, clutching the other's shoulders. "Now, go knock it out of the park."

"Thank you. Thank you for everything." Long curly hair flew behind her as Carmen ran to the door of the closest shop, offering the briefest of waves before disappearing inside.

Matt's gaze jumped back to the blonde. He caught the end of her wide smile, which sent his pulse skittering as if he'd just run five miles in the sand. The wind picked up a strand of her hair and the hem of her green skirt, but she wrestled them both back into place, never taking her eyes off the closed door.

She blinked long lashes, her smile settling from pure joy into pride as he drew even with her and caught a glimpse of stunning blue eyes. *Familiar* blue eyes. It couldn't be. There was no way this woman was Tristan's little sister.

Her eyebrows rose suddenly. "Matt?"

He stopped in midstride, his smile growing slowly. "Ashley?"

All of a sudden she threw her arms around his shoulders, hugging him as though she'd never quit. She must have been nearly on her toes to reach that high. He awkwardly patted her back. Ashley was the closest thing he'd ever had to a little sister, but he was out of practice. He hadn't seen her in more than four years. In fact, the last time he'd seen her, she was more teenager than woman. And SEAL training didn't include continuing courses in relating to your best friend's kid sister.

She rocked back on her heels, her eyes glowing. "I thought you were injured. Tristan called and said… Are you all right?" Her nose wrinkled as she squinted her eyes to narrow their focus on his.

Could she see straight through him with that gaze? His stomach twisted, and he bit his tongue to keep from laughing at the way she looked at once very childlike—freckles still paraded over her nose—and all grown-up. Finally he replied, "I'll live."

She rolled her eyes and shook her head. "Have it your way." She glanced down the sidewalk and then back to the door behind him. "I'm in town to run some errands. Can you join me?"

"Sure. I'd love to."

She nodded to the pharmacy behind her. "I have to pick up a prescription." As she led him down an aisle toward the back counter, she shot him a dazzling smile. "I'm so happy to see you, but what on earth are you doing here? Tristan made some joke about sending you here to recuperate, but I thought he was just kidding."

He shoved his hands into the pockets of his jeans and prayed she wouldn't be upset. He remembered a fight she'd had with Tristan during Matt's first visit to their home. Tristan had tried to get her to break up with her boyfriend. Sixteen-year-old Ashley hadn't appreciated Tristan sticking his nose in her business. But maybe that had changed in eight years.

"Your brother *did* send me…but not to recuperate."

Her eyebrows pinched together as she turned to accept a bottle of pink syrup from the white-coated pharmacist. "Thank you." She tipped a smile to the man on the other side of the counter, but when she turned back to Matt, her face was filled with questions, although she asked only one. "Why did he send you, then?"

"He was worried. Said your mom called him, too."

She looked up into the fluorescent lights and crossed her arms before picking up a wire basket at the end of one of the aisles and tossing a bag of Christmas ribbons into it. "It's really not a big deal. I wish you'd just called instead of wasting a trip up here."

"What happened?" His knee buckled as he took a step to follow her, and he silently chastised it, hating every moment that his body didn't perform at its peak.

"You first." She picked up two tubes of antibacterial ointment but glanced pointedly at his leg.

"Nothing."

"Liar."

He chuckled as she put her basket down on the counter and the cashier began ringing up her items. "Fine. I ran into a guy with a knife. Ended up with a few stitches."

The cashier shot him a curious stare, but Ashley only handed her the cash to pay for her purchases before leading him toward the door.

"You make it sound like nothing, but I know it's not."

She clearly had all sorts of questions, but he didn't have any answers for them. That mission was classified, and even if it wasn't, he wasn't going to tell her he'd saved her brother from a guy with an eight-inch blade. She had enough on her plate without adding on more fears for her brother. He'd protected his best friend—that was what mattered. And now he was going to protect his friend's sister.

They stepped out onto the sidewalk, and she let him carry the bags as they strolled around the corner to a small secondhand clothing store.

When it was clear that she wasn't going to fill in the blanks in her own story without prompting, he figured that the best strategy would be to charge right in. "So what happened that has your mom so worried that she called and riled up your brother?"

Ashley ducked behind a circular rack of sweaters, blocking her face by holding up a top that should have only been worn by traffic cones. "Nothing worth making this much of a fuss about."

"You're bad at this."

The sweater dropped, revealing rows of parallel wrinkles on her forehead and shining eyes. "Shopping?"

He didn't back down from the intensity of her gaze. "Dodging the question." The room was so full that he had to slide between the overstuffed racks like a sand snake to reach her side. Without drawing undue attention from the pair of women on the far side of the store, he leaned in so that she couldn't look away. When she blinked up at him with ocean-blue eyes and tucked her bottom lip between her teeth, his stomach lurched. "Tristan is the closest thing to a brother I've ever had. He's worried about you, and so am I. I promised him I'd check in on you. Let me help."

Fear flickered through her eyes, and she broke eye contact, taking the moment to hang the orange monstrosity back on its hanger, which seemed to take a lot longer than it should.

Matt couldn't do his job if he couldn't read body language, and right now hers was telling him that she felt she was in over her head. Something *had* happened to put her in danger, even if she didn't want to admit it. The direct approach hadn't worked—maybe he could ease her into it, if he could get her talking.

"Tristan tells me that you're running a battered women's shelter."

"That's right."

He caught her gaze as she picked up several tops at least two sizes too big for her. "He brags about you all the time. Tells us how smart and talented you are." She looked away. He'd stepped over the line. She may have been like a little sister, but it didn't mean he knew her well enough to gush like he had. Time to get the conversation back on track. "But he says that not everyone is happy with the work that you're doing. That sometimes the husbands and boyfriends of the women you're helping get angry. Make threats. Maybe even…attack you directly."

Still not meeting his gaze again, she whispered, "Someone wasn't paying attention and almost ran me over." She ran her fingers over the hangers on the metal frame, studying the shirts as though there would be a test on them later. "It just rattled me a bit, but I'm sure it was just an accident now."

"Tristan said something about a letter," Matt pressed.

Ashley nodded, examining a stain on the front of one of the shirts. Frowning, she put it back and picked up another. "When I got home that day, there was an anonymous note saying that someone wanted his property back."

"You get a lot of anonymous letters?"

Her nod was slow and thoughtful. "I suppose. More than a normal person."

His gut clenched. What kind of jerk threatened a battered women's shelter? Someone without any respect. And a man who didn't respect women could be dangerous. "Was there anything that made you think that particular note was connected to the car that almost hit you?" He followed her to shelves piled with blue jeans.

"Ye-es," she said slowly. "That is, I thought there was at the time. The note said something about missing me—that even though he'd missed me, I shouldn't think that that meant I could keep his property. But maybe he just meant he'd missed seeing me—that he'd come by the house when I wasn't there for him to yell at me in person."

"Did you turn the note over to the police?"

The glance over her shoulder at him was more resigned than worried.

Had threats become such a part of her life at Lil's Place that she couldn't even recognize a real one when it came along?

And this one was real.

"Of course I did. The chief told me they couldn't do anything. The threat was too vague. It wasn't...well... threatening enough."

Matt subdued the growl growing at the back of his throat. Abusive men weren't to be trifled with. They weren't concerned about anyone but themselves. Matt knew that firsthand. He also knew that they didn't give up. If this guy was angry enough to try to run Ashley over, he wasn't going to give up if she didn't capitulate after a note. This guy would try other, more forceful tactics until he got what he wanted.

Maybe he hadn't always been able to protect his foster moms from being beaten when he was a kid, but he most certainly could do something to protect Ashley from an abuser now. Ten years on the teams and more training than any man could use at one time, he knew how to defend himself and how to protect the innocent. And with her platinum-blond hair, freckled nose and shining eyes, she looked like the epitome of innocence.

"Listen, I'm just going to be in town for a few days. I'm already set up at the hotel down the street. Let me just look into things while I'm here." He followed her to the register as she purchased several pairs of jeans. "I won't get in your way."

She smiled up at him as though he was a child. "Thanks, but I'm okay. Really. I'm used to taking care of my girls." She stepped through the door that he held open and strolled toward her parked car. "I got the note more than a week ago. If there was any danger, something else would have happened by now." She laughed up at him, her eyes crinkling at the corners. "So now what will you do?"

He pushed her arm as he'd seen Tristan do a thousand times, pushing aside a decidedly unbrotherly thought. "Well, my hotel doesn't have ESPN, but I am trained in spec ops. I'll come up with something."

Something like setting up a perimeter around her home to keep the threat at bay, and making sure that her security system would do its job. He'd stop by the police station and see if he could get them to pay a little more attention to Ashley's situation, just in case he needed them down the road. And then he'd ask around to see if there were any troublemakers in town. Pressing on them might reveal the coward afraid to stand by his threats.

As they reached her car, her laughter died on her lips. He didn't have to ask if she still thought the threat had passed. Pure terror flashed across her face as she took in the smashed windshield of her coupe. And tucked over a spiderweb of cracks and under a wiper blade, the person responsible for the mess had left a clear message.

If I don't get what's mine, you'll get what's yours.

TWO

Crossing her arms against a chill coming from somewhere deep within, Ashley stared at the note still wedged beneath the wiper blade.

If I don't get what's mine, you'll get what's yours.

Another line beneath the first gave instructions for returning his property. *Put it back where you found it.*

The words made her skin crawl as another shiver shot down her spine, causing the hairs on her arms to stand on end. Her gaze traveled up and down the sidewalk. The chalkboard signs and colorful awnings were the only signs of life, except for Matt, who was marching backward toward the closest alley, his eyes squinting at her hard. "Stay put."

At any other time, she might have resented being ordered around, but at that moment she was too worried to even notice. Apparently the note and near hit-and-run hadn't been a fluke. Someone really was after something. Or someone.

And that meant she might need the SEAL's help to protect her girls. As uncomfortable as she was with the thought of trusting her safety—and especially the safety of the families in her house—to someone else, her discomfort seemed a small price for the specialized protection he could offer.

She pressed her hands to her cheeks and took several deep breaths, her stomach pitching like a canoe in a typhoon. Even with her eyes pinched closed, she could see her windshield, and she clamped them even tighter, trying to dispel the image. Although the picture wouldn't disappear, she refused to give in to the burning at the back of her eyes, instead letting out a slow breath through clenched teeth as she prayed for something she couldn't even name.

Peace?

Courage?

Protection?

"There's no one there." Matt's words snatched her from the depths of her own mind. "This must have happened a while ago." His lips barely moved, but the force of his tone could have blown over the first little pig's house. She could only be thankful that his ire was directed at the situation and not at her.

"Thanks for checking."

"We need to report this."

She nodded, reaching into her purse and pulling out her phone. "First I have to call the house and make sure everyone's okay. That this guy—" she nodded toward her car "—didn't go there after doing this." With fingers that shook more than she wanted to admit, she punched in the number to Lil's Place; the knot in her stomach tightened with each unanswered ring.

The intensity in Matt's eyes only made her throat thick, so she turned her back on him. Holding her breath on the fifth ring, she prayed someone would pick up. What if the man who'd smashed her windshield and left this note had hurt the women at Lil's?

No. She wouldn't let that happen. Not on her watch.

If someone didn't answer on the next ring, she'd fly— shattered glass and all—back to the house.

"Hello?"

"Meghan?"

"Hi, Ashley." Was her voice too calm? Her tone overly cool? Was someone there with her, threatening her?

Ashley bit her lip hard, the pain forcing her mind back to the immediate. "Is everything all right at the house?"

"Of course."

"But it took five rings for you to pick up."

Meghan chuckled, the bright, cheerful sound an exact replica of her ten-year-old daughter's laugh. "The girls and I are making cookies, and we had the mixer on. We didn't hear the phone."

"And everyone else? Carmen? Benita and Julio?"

"Well, Carmen left this morning with you, but everyone else is in the living room." Right. Carmen's interview and testing for the bookkeeping position would last at least another couple of hours, and she had lined up another ride back to Lil's.

Meghan's tone dropped, and Ashley could picture her ducking into the hallway away from her two young daughters. "What's going on? Are *you* all right?"

Ashley let out a slow breath, glancing back at the car and the intimidating man leaning against it. Arms crossed, he leaned on one leg and rested the other foot on top of the opposite ankle, his eyes sweeping the street over and over. When he caught her staring at him, he gave her a quick nod and returned to his watching.

"Yes, yes. Everything's fine. I'll be home soon."

"All right. Bye, then."

Ashley pressed the button on her phone to end the call and slipped it back into her purse. The hair on her arms was just beginning to fall back into place.

She turned to call to Matt, only to find him already at her side, the offending note gripped between two gloved fingers. "Ready?" He nodded toward the police station across the street and fell into step beside her.

It took all of Matt's willpower not to run to the police station and demand to know why they hadn't done more to protect Ashley and her charges. How could the cops let a car be vandalized right across the street from their station? He took a deep breath and forced himself to calm down. For all intents and purposes, he was a civilian here with no authority. And the police wouldn't be willing to work with him if he charged in, taking over the situation.

He could sit back this time. Watch and listen. Any mission was doomed to fail if there wasn't enough intel. Time for a little recon.

As they entered the fluorescent light of the station, Ashley's back arched a fraction, her pointed chin sticking out just a little bit farther, and he couldn't help his smile as she approached the unassuming officer standing behind the counter.

"I'd like to speak with the chief." Ashley's voice, completely even and free of any hint of the scare she'd just received, carried to every corner of the room. If the chief was in, he'd heard her.

"I'm sorry." The officer folded his newspaper and set it on the counter, smoothing it out with a single swipe. "The chief isn't in right now."

Ashley leaned in a little more, her eyes unblinking. "Well, then, who can I speak with about my smashed windshield and the threatening note left under my wiper? Perhaps you're available to take a look at it?"

"Sorry. I'm the only one here, and I can't leave." The burly desk sergeant flipped his hand toward the two chairs on the opposite side of the room. "But you can wait here for the chief if you want to."

Ashley's shoulders dropped a fraction, but she marched over to the chairs as though this was why she'd come to the station. Matt couldn't match her nonchalance; his frown was still on display. When they were settled into the seats, he bent toward her. "Is it usually like this?"

"Small town. Small police force." She never took her gaze from the sergeant—at least, what was visible of the top of his head behind the paper he'd resumed reading. "The chief knows my situation, but he's still only one guy."

The police might not be much help. Matt had hoped that they would be halfway to identifying the threat to Ashley by now. But if the local law enforcement wasn't equipped to do that, it was up to him. Which meant he needed information and a place to start. No time like the present.

"So who do you think tried to run you over last week?"

Taking an audible breath, she sat a little taller in her chair. "Like I said before, we get calls and threats at Lil's Place. It's just part of the job. Ex-husbands. Soon-to-be exes. Boyfriends. We've heard from them all. But we hadn't had anything significant for a few weeks before last. Of course, we hadn't had any new residents for a while up until last week. But there's something different about these threats."

"How so?"

She folded her hands in her lap, every inch the calm and collected professional until her knuckles turned white. She squeezed them so hard that the tips of her fingers turned red; she seemed wound tighter than a guitar string. But at least he could help her. He'd do whatever it took to make sure that Ashley—and anyone that she called family— was safe from whatever goon lurked in the shadows. He owed that to Ashley and her mother, who'd welcomed him into their family—and he owed even more to Tristan, who would never forgive him if anything happened to Ashley on his watch.

"Usually we know exactly who the threats are from. Abusive husbands aren't usually afraid of being recognized." She glanced into his eyes as she chewed on her lower lip. "These notes are different. They're so vague. No names. No precise demands. They could be from anyone."

Matt finally set the note from her windshield down on the table next to his bouncing knee. "And you haven't seen anyone lurking around your place?"

Instead of answering his question, Ashley jumped up as two men entered the station. "Chief Donal, may I speak with you?"

So this was the missing chief.

"Hello, there, Miss Sawyer." As he turned back to his companion, his sport coat pulled tight against his round belly, and he unbuttoned the jacket. "I'll see you for lunch tomorrow, Jimmy. Same time?"

Jimmy nodded and waved, but not before tipping his nonexistent hat at Ashley. He didn't bother with more than a glance in Matt's direction before disappearing out the door. Matt didn't like a guy who didn't at least acknowledge another man, but there wasn't time to dwell on it as he gave the police chief his full attention.

"Well, well. Miss Sawyer. Twice in one week? What have I done to deserve such a treat? And you've brought a friend." Donal stuck his hand out. "Albert Donal, police chief."

Matt stood slowly, careful not to favor his injured leg. It wouldn't do to have anyone thinking he wasn't up to his assignment. He squeezed the other man's hand just hard enough to let the chief know he wasn't dealing with a pushover. "Senior Chief Matt Waterstone."

Donal pulled his hand back, nodding. "A navy man."

Ashley clearly had no time for formalities; she stepped directly in front of the older man. "Someone smashed in my windshield and left me another note."

Using a gloved hand to make sure he didn't leave fingerprints on the note, Matt held it out to the chief.

Donal's eyes narrowed, and he ushered them into his office. He produced an evidence bag and slipped the scrap of paper inside.

When he had settled into the leather chair behind his wide desk, the police chief studied the paper. "Where'd the note come from?" He didn't tear his gaze from the message, as though studying it would reveal some sort of hidden meaning.

"It was under my windshield wiper."

Donal glanced up then, surprise crossing his features. "Sit down. Please."

They accepted the offer, both leaning toward the chief.

"Did you see who left this or what smashed your windshield?"

Matt looked at Ashley, but she didn't wait for him before diving in. "We were running a few errands—to Puckett's Pharmacy and Jenni's shop—and when we came back, someone had smashed it and left the note."

"Whoa, there." Donal held up both hands. "We don't know that the same person who wrote the note also smashed your windshield. For that matter, we don't know that the broken windshield wasn't an accident of some sort. We have had an increase in vandalism since the layoffs at the plant. It might even just be kids playing a prank."

"You think this is kids?" Matt couldn't keep the astonishment out of his voice. "Kids didn't leave that note. And what are the chances that someone would leave a note for Ashley and someone else would randomly vandalize her car all on the same day? That's some coincidence, don't you think?"

The chief looked directly into his eyes, something the older man hadn't done so far. "I hear what you're saying, but this note isn't much to go on. I can't assume anything without real evidence." He looked sincere, as though he wished he had different news. "In and of itself, this note wouldn't even hold up in court."

Ashley's nose wrinkled at this bit of news. "So you're saying that that—" she swung her finger toward the plastic bag still in Donal's hand "—isn't dangerous enough? Someone who's willing to use violence to make a point could be after one of my girls, and this isn't enough of a threat?"

"That's right." He held it out to her, so that both Matt and Ashley could read the words typed there.

Not that Matt needed another look. Those words had been seared into his memory from the moment he read them. He didn't see how they could be read as anything other than intimidation toward Ashley and someone else at Lil's Place.

The chief continued, "Yes, it could be construed as threatening. But it could also just be a reminder that someone wants his lawnmower back."

"I have my own lawnmower."

"That's not the point. It could be anything that's been borrowed from a neighbor." Donal ran his hand over his grease-slicked hair. "The point is, the burden of proof on these things is on us. Even if we figured out who was behind this, the newest lawyer in the public defender's office could get the writer of either of your notes free. And because there's nothing here that confirms violent intent, my hands are tied."

Ashley opened her mouth to speak, but Matt cut her off

with a hand on her shoulder. "Will you at least look into it? Check for fingerprints?"

"Absolutely." The round man heaved himself from his burgundy leather chair, his stance a silent invitation for them to leave. "Tell you what. I'll ask my guy Frank to drive past Lil's Place a few times a day and keep an eye out for anything suspicious."

Matt stood, reaching for Ashley's elbow, but she beat him out of her chair, offering her hand and a half smile to the chief. "I'd appreciate anything you can do."

Before either of them could say something else, Donal looked hard at them. "Let my guys do their jobs. Don't get in our way. We'll handle this."

Matt bit the inside of his cheek and forced a smile. "Thank you, Chief."

They weren't going to get any more of a commitment from the police force than that, and it would only hurt Ashley's case to be at odds with them.

As they stepped back into the afternoon sunshine, Ashley shot him a glance through narrowed eyes, her nose wrinkled and lips pursed. "What do you think?"

He shot her a smile. "I think we're going to have to fly under the radar."

"What does that mean?" But the flash of her grin told him she already knew.

"Someone thinks they only have to contend with the Charity Way Police Department. They're in for a nasty surprise."

Ashley frowned. "What if Chief Donal is right? I mean, this all could just be a misunderstanding."

Of course she'd say something like that. She wanted a fight with an unknown threat about as much as she wanted that shattered windshield. But wanting the fight and getting it anyway were two different things.

"Are you willing to take a chance like that—not just for yourself, but for the families at the shelter?" He was manipulating her, but he couldn't bring himself to care. She might take chances with her own safety, but she'd never risk anyone at Lil's Place. The only way to keep her safe was to remind her that she wasn't the only one at risk.

"You're right," she said with a sigh. "We'll do things your way—for now." Matt noted the clear warning in her glare but chose not to respond. He couldn't argue with her, not when he needed her cooperation. Her knowledge was his only chance at identifying the threat. This wasn't his usual assignment—he had no mission parameters, no assigned and carefully researched target, no backup from his team.

And with Ashley at stake, there was absolutely no room for failure.

THREE

Ashley blinked against the sun reflecting off the spider-web of her windshield, hands on the wheel and chin on her chest. Who would do such a thing? And why? Abuse usually took place behind closed doors, when there was no one around to witness it. Abusers were very, very good at protecting themselves from the consequences of their violence. An open attack like this seemed so strange, so out of character. And that made her nervous. If her attacker was willing to go this far, what would he do next?

She rolled her window down as Matt leaned a forearm on the roof of the car, towering over her little coupe.

"Do you want to leave the car here and call a tow truck? I can drive you back to your place."

She managed to offer him a slightly off-center smile. "I'm okay. I won't run anyone over. I promise. The glass place is right around the corner." And there was no way she could afford to pay for a tow truck either. But he didn't need to know that.

"You sure? You'll be driving right into the sun. It could be kind of hard to see. Would you rather drive my truck?"

She glanced down the street at the SEAL-approved vehicle of choice. The truck was tall enough to accommodate his long legs, but not so big that it drew undo attention.

Besides, she didn't need him to hold her hand in this. She'd accept his help safeguarding Lil's Place—he was much better qualified in that arena. But driving her car a couple of blocks wasn't a mission only a SEAL could do. He was capable, but so was she. "That's all right. I'd rather drive mine."

"Fair enough."

Why did his words sound just the opposite?

"I'm fine. Really."

"If you're sure." She nodded. "Okay. I'll follow you over there, and then take you home."

"Thanks. I appreciate the ride."

"I won't leave you stranded." There was something deeper to his words, like he was going to give her more than a ride. Like he was promising to see her through this whole ordeal.

Even if she didn't need it. She'd been just fine on her own for the last three years.

She glanced up just in time to catch Matt's reflection in the rearview mirror as he walked behind her car toward his truck. He favored his left leg ever so slightly, his gait just a bit off, but despite his uneven stride, he was in his truck and pulling out of his parking spot—leaving room for her to pull out in front of him—before she'd even turned her car on.

As she pulled into the empty street, the cracks turned her windshield into a kaleidoscope, which proved harder to see through than she had anticipated. She fought to stay between the barely visible lane lines.

"Just keep going straight." She repeated the mantra several times before another driver blasted his horn at her for crossing the middle line. She swerved back into her own lane, drawing dangerously close to a car parked along the curb.

Her breathing picked up speed to match her pulse until she pulled into the gravel parking lot of the glass-repair shop.

True to his word, Matt came in right behind her, parking beside her coupe as she ducked into the front office.

Ten minutes later she hurried up to Matt's truck, clutching her purse. Getting up to the seat could have been part of a training regimen to climb Everest.

"Need a hand?" Matt turned to open his own door, but she clawed at the bench seat until she gained enough of a grip to scramble all the way up.

"Nope. I've got it."

He nodded, slamming his door closed at the same time she settled into her seat, hands clasped in her lap.

"Where to?"

She directed him toward Lil's Place and settled in. The heater kicked out lukewarm air, taking the chill out of the Northern California winter afternoon. She rubbed her hands together and held them in front of the vents.

"What did they say?"

She sighed. "They're closed tomorrow, and they have a backlog. So it'll take at least a couple days. They said they hope it'll be done by Saturday morning."

He frowned, his eyebrows pinching together. "That seems like a long time for you to be without a car. I'm not sure it's safe for you not to have one."

"Maybe that was his plan." She said the words without really thinking, but they rang true.

The truck rumbled along, filling the silence, and she knew he recognized the truth of it as well. "I'll be in town for a while. I'll take you anywhere you need to go."

She smiled, really looking at him for the first time since

she'd run into him that morning. His jacket hung open, and his snug T-shirt revealed that the man didn't have an ounce of fat on him, despite his injury. The loose curls on top of his head that might have made another man look boyish, just made Matt look like the statues of Greek gods she'd studied in art history.

His presence was reassuring at the least. And strangely familiar, even if she hadn't seen him for more than four years. Matt had accompanied Tristan home for Christmas that year, and, at barely twenty, she'd had a bit of a crush on him. That was before Paul had come into her life.

She'd never been sure if Matt had been aware of her feelings for him back then. Of course, when they started, she'd been just sixteen. That had been more schoolgirl crush than full-on attraction. With time, and increased maturity, her feelings had grown. But Matt had either never realized or never acknowledged her interest in him. In the handful of times he'd visited their home during her senior year of high school, he'd teased her just like Tristan. Just one of the family.

She'd never told her mom—let alone Tristan—how much she liked Matt back then.

And then Paul happened.

So exciting at first. Rappelling and midnight swimming in the lake. He drove fast and broke the rules, ditched class and stayed up all night talking with her.

Despite Tristan's warnings that Paul might not be everything he seemed, she'd fallen for him. Hard.

Just as hard as his fist the first time he had hit her.

She hadn't thought romantically about any man since Paul. Not Matt or anyone else.

But now that Matt was here, sitting next to her and filling the cab more than he should have, her mind wandered to the past and dug up memories that had no place in her current situation.

In the edge of her line of sight, he twisted, rubbing his calf. She'd never seen him fidget before, but every time she ventured a glance in his direction, he shifted, turning his body toward her, but his leg away.

"Your leg bothering you?"

"Not really."

"I thought they taught you to be better liars in SEAL training."

This whipped his gaze in her direction, and it landed heavily on her face. But a quick glance his way revealed an accompanying grin. It was lopsided and immensely endearing, despite her desire to think of him as nothing more than an extra set of hands to protect her charges.

"So what's for dinner at Lil's tonight?"

Ashley shot him a pointed look, and the corners of his mouth arched into an even wider smile, forming almost-dimples to his jawline. He was far too charming for his own good. It was distracting, which would have been dangerous enough at any time. Just now, when she needed all of her wits about her, it could be disastrous. Was it really safer for everyone involved—especially her—to let him help with this situation?

"I'm not sure. Why?"

"Thought you might invite me to join you."

"Whoa." She held up her hands. "That's a bad idea. Very bad idea."

"Why's that?"

She studied the small black purse in her hands, turning it over several times, hoping it would give her the right words. "It's just that the women at Lil's have had hard lives, been treated horribly by the men they trusted. I try not to bring guys into the house unless absolutely necessary."

"Don't you think this might be absolutely necessary?"

"What? Feeding you dinner?"

He pulled up to a red light and turned his head to look into her eyes. She blinked twice but forced herself to maintain eye contact. "Listen, Ashley, you don't have to act like this with me." She almost asked what he meant, but she already knew. "You're in trouble. You and the girls at Lil's. Until this letter-writing lunatic is caught, someone needs to watch your back. And your brother asked me for a favor. We've been watching out for each other since day one of BUD/S, and I'm not going to let him down. He's the only family I've got."

She already knew that Tristan and Matt had met on the first day of BUD/S—Basic Underwater Demolition/SEAL training. But how did Matt not have any other family? He'd visited their home for years, but he'd never really talked about his own background. Tristan had always been the talker, and early on, he'd told her not to grill Matt about why he wasn't going home for the holidays. She hadn't cared, really. She had just wanted Matt to keep coming back to the house. But had he really never mentioned his family?

Before she could ask, Matt leaned toward her, his face drawing nearer to hers, setting her heart thumping painfully. He took a deep breath, his shoulders rising and nostrils flaring slightly as he let it out. "That makes you family, too. So I'm going to be in Charity Way until I'm certain that you're absolutely safe."

His tone brooked no argument, but a second later, the fierce intensity gave way to the serene calm she expected from him. He turned his eyes back to the road and pressed the accelerator. "It's just dinner. I promise not to scare anyone."

Didn't he realize he was already scaring *her?*

She'd already relied on him more than she had any man since Paul, letting him make her feel safe just by standing next to her. She already hated the thought of him leaving, the thought of losing his steadying presence in the midst of something she couldn't explain or understand.

And for someone with her history, that was the scariest thought of all.

Apparently Matt had said the right thing.

Ashley nodded but changed the subject, diving into the discussion of possible threats. "The notes have to be connected to one of the women at Lil's Place." Ashley's teeth found her lower lip, chewing away. "They refer to someone's property. That's got to be one of the women."

"Probably. But just for the sake of argument, could it be personal against you, since the house hasn't been targeted yet? Have you had any personal arguments or disagreements with anyone lately?"

"Of course not. I'm far too sweet for that."

He shot her a raised eyebrow.

Ashley laughed behind her hand. "Fine. But I'm not usually one to pick a fight. Besides, I'm usually busy taking care of things at the house, so outside of running errands and going to church, I'm hardly ever in town."

"So you haven't had any run-ins with anyone in the last month or so?"

"Most people in this town leave me and Lil's Place alone. We've had a few vocal citizens who think we should stay out of other people's business. But they're pretty few and far between. We have a couple regular volunteers, and Chief Donal notes all of my concerns, but other than that, we're a quiet house on a block with a bunch of other quiet houses."

"What about friends? People at church? Has anyone seemed strange lately?"

She pursed her lips to the side, her nose wrinkling as she thought out loud. "Well, Miranda's been a bit more scatterbrained than usual."

"Who's Miranda?"

"She's a volunteer and a friend of mine." Ashley's head swiveled to watch a green station wagon roll past them before continuing. "She missed two volunteer kitchen shifts last week, but she said that work has been crazy lately. The tire plant had layoffs and she works in human resources there."

"What about a boyfriend? Are you seeing anyone?"

She wanted to tell him it was none of his business. It was written all over her face. But she wrapped her arms around her stomach instead. "Nothing serious."

She wasn't telling the whole truth. He could read that like a book, too. And for some reason, being questioned about a boyfriend made her uncomfortable. Bad breakup? No, she'd admit to that—she wouldn't hold back if there was a chance her ex was involved. So what was the problem?

He wanted to question her further, but she seemed so tense that he decided to let it drop. For now.

Swallowing back his questions and pushing all thoughts of Ashley's love life out of his mind, he navigated their conversation back on course. "So if it is related to one of the women at the house, who do you think it might be?"

"That's the problem—I think it might be related to a girl who's *not* in the house anymore. She's the only one whose background is a mystery."

"She wouldn't tell you?"

"She wouldn't say much more than her name—Joy. And she promised she was eighteen, but she looked like she was barely sixteen." Lines appeared on Ashley's face, making her look much older than her years. She couldn't be much more than twenty-five, but the pain in her eyes added at least ten years.

"How did she end up at Lil's?"

Ashley motioned to the next street, indicating that he should turn there. And just as she'd said, it was a street of ordinary two-story houses all with white porches and the occasional porch swing. All they needed were white picket fences to complete his childhood daydream of the perfect home.

"Miranda brought her about a week ago. She said she didn't know the girl very well, but she knew Joy needed help."

Ashley pointed at a yellow house, and he pulled into an open spot at the curb adjacent to the green lawn.

"It must have been bad," she continued.

He turned the key in the ignition, twisting toward her. "What?"

Ashley turned toward the house and opened the door before responding. "Whatever Joy went through. Whoever she's running from did a number on her, and she wouldn't talk about it. At all."

He hurried around the hood of the truck, heat still rising from it, to meet her at the foot of the path leading up to the front steps.

After several seconds of silence, he held out his hand, motioning her to take the lead, but she shook her head. "We need to figure out what we're going to tell everyone."

Matt frowned. "Tell them about what?"

"About why you're here."

Matt still didn't follow. His confusion must have been clear on his face, because Ashley continued, "The women inside that house trust me to keep them safe. I

can't just bring a strange—" her eyes dropped to his tennis shoes then moved all the way back up to the top of
his hair "—man into their haven."

"Then we'll explain to them that I'm here for their protection."

Her voice dropped to a whisper without any change in
conviction. "And what? Tell them that I'm being threatened? That's not going to make them feel secure, and security is essential for the residents of Lil's Place."

Matt rubbed his palms across the legs of his jeans. "I
don't like this any more than you, but you're in danger.
You're *all* in danger. Until we nail this guy, every woman
inside that house is a potential target. Even if this guy is
only after you, I'd imagine everyone in town knows that
hurting one of your girls is the best way to hurt you. So
you and I need to make sure that your home and its residents are safe. We can keep them from becoming prey."

"But—"

"I'm going to check the windows to make sure they're
locked and that the locks work. I'm going to look at the
doors to make sure they're sturdy. And then I'm going to
go back to my hotel." The urge to validate his statements
with physical contact struck, and he went with it, resting
his hand on her upper arm.

He could have wrapped his fingers all the way around
her biceps if he'd tried. She really was much smaller than
she came across, all gumption and guts.

Her eyes turned hard and then softer, and he'd have
given anything to be able to read her mind. Instead he
prayed that she'd consent. This was the first step to protecting Ashley. The first step to finding the man behind
the notes.

Finally she nodded. "All right. But you'll stay by me
the whole time."

He'd do whatever it took to find the creep responsible. And staying by Ashley's side while he was at it? He'd never had a sweeter assignment.

As they stepped from the dim front step into the bright foyer, Ashley worried on her bottom lip. Had she done the right thing letting Matt into Lil's? Would he frighten women already traumatized by men they'd trusted?

On the verge of changing her mind, she ran into Benita, a young mom. "Ashley! You have to see—" Her voice died on her lips as she spied Matt, still standing behind Ashley.

Should she introduce Matt or demand to know what had sent Benita into such a frenzy? Deciding Matt could wait, she stepped directly in front of the woman and grabbed her hands. "What's going on? What's happened?"

Benita's gaze swept back to Ashley's face. "It's not that important."

"Of course it is. What's wrong?"

Matching pink spots appeared on her olive cheeks. "It's really nothing...I just finished knitting Julio's sweater."

Ashley patted Benita's hands, her voice rising. "I'd love to see it! But first—" she nodded behind her "—this is my friend Matt."

Suddenly his arm snaked around her, hand outstretched to Benita, whose wide, unblinking eyes never left Matt's face. Ashley twisted to get a better view of him, and when she did, her breath caught in her throat. All traces of determination had vanished. In its place was a smile so gentle and serene that she'd have let him into her home without question.

And Benita responded to it. Unclenching her fists, she slipped her hand into his much larger one. "Matt Waterstone, ma'am. It's a pleasure to meet you."

Caution and trust battled across Benita's face before

she bowed her head and murmured an unintelligible response. When she lifted her head, her smile reached the whole way across her face.

"Did you say you'd finished knitting a sweater?" Matt continued talking, keeping her between him and Benita. "Could we see it?"

Benita's eyes shone with something akin to pride. Something that had been missing since her arrival. She motioned for them to follow her into the living room, where a boy and two girls played on the carpet.

All three looked up from their game as the adults walked in, and Ashley made quick introductions, pointing out and naming each of the children. "Julio, Greta, Sara, this is my friend Matt."

Again he offered that smile. The one that belied that he was a warrior, trained to do his job better than nearly anyone else on the planet. The one that made her stomach roll ever so slightly.

Suddenly he dropped to his knees next to the children's board game and drew even with the smallest child. "Can I join you, Greta?"

The little girl tucked her chin in, but looked up at him through enormous blue eyes. Her bright red pigtails fell over her shoulders as her tiny fingers placed the dice into Matt's weathered ones. He winked at the little girl and asked how to play the game just as Lil Kitrick entered, eyeing him with concern.

With shuffling steps she approached Matt, who popped to his feet, appearing at least twice Lil's size. "Ma'am." He held out his hand to shake hers. "Matt Waterstone."

"Lillian. But everyone 'round here calls me Lil."

His smile competed with the lights adorning the Christmas tree in the corner. "This must be your place."

She nodded. "It was. It's more Ashley's now. But she does let me stay here."

Ashley walked up behind her mentor, putting a hand on her shoulder. "Lil, you're too humble, as usual. We couldn't do any of this without you."

After a few more words, Lil seemed to give her approval of Matt and moved to her rocking chair in the corner to knit. Matt dropped back to the floor and picked up the game with the kids.

She could have watched them play for hours, and she might have if Benita hadn't drawn her to the couch, where a slightly uneven sweater lay over the arm.

The evening passed like a flash, the dinner table surrounded by curious glances toward their visitor. But it was Julio, sitting next to Matt, who finally asked the lingering question. "Why are you here?"

The boy's mother looked as if she could fall out of her chair, hushing Julio with fluttering hands. But Matt gave the boy a lopsided grin, chewing slowly on a bite of dinner. Ashley chomped on her own mouthful, trying to beat him to the answer, but the baked chicken lodged in her throat.

After a quick swallow, Matt said, "I came into town to visit Ashley, and heard about some petty crime in town. Thought I could stop by and double-check that all your locks are working right."

"Can I go with you?" Julio bounced in his chair, dropping his fork to the floor with a clatter. "Please."

"Finish your chow first, and then I don't see why not."

By the time the meal was over and Matt had taken Julio and Benita around to each room, showing them how to test to make sure the window locks were secure, it was nearly ten.

Ashley turned off the security alarm and opened the front door to let Matt step onto the front stoop. As she did, a chill ran down her spine like the weight of someone's gaze heavy on her shoulders. She couldn't make out any shapes in the darkness and decided the chill must have been caused by the cool evening air.

"We found a couple broken window locks, and the chain on the front door isn't going to keep out more than a tomcat." Matt stopped and looked over his shoulder in the same direction she'd glanced a moment before. He turned back to her with a furrowed brow, but he didn't say anything about it. She wondered if he'd felt the same thing she had. "I'll be back in the morning to fix those."

"Thank you, Matt." Without even realizing it, she put her hand on his arm, and the muscles below his jacket sleeve rippled at just her touch. Jerking back, she tried to cover her action. "You were great with the kids tonight."

"Anytime." His voice trailed off as he turned to peer over his shoulder again. "Are you expecting anyone tonight?"

"No." She fought another chill. "Is there… Do you feel like someone's out there?"

Matt's head bobbed very slowly as his eyes traveled back and forth, scanning the lawn. Suddenly his eyes narrowed, a muscle in his jaw jumped and his fists clenched. "Stay inside and lock the door. Don't open it for anyone but me."

Her objection died on her lips as a man in black materialized near the corner of her lawn.

FOUR

Matt growled deep in his throat, his knee screaming as he sailed across the lawn toward the figure still in shadows. This could be the guy who had threatened Ashley. This was his chance to pin down the jerk and get some answers.

It was dumb. Careless. Amateurish. The porch was well-lit, and the guy was watching it closely. He should have pretended to leave and snuck around behind the guy, but it was too late now. As soon as Matt moved toward him, the man in black noticed and ran, too. His pace was no match for a SEAL running at top speed, but he had a pretty major head start. He hit the sidewalk seconds ahead of Matt, diving into a car idling at the curb.

Matt ran into the street, but was met only by the blaring horn and blinding lights of the car as it took off. He bounced off the offending hood and managed to land on steady feet.

Ashley ran up behind him as the car sailed away.

Probably a getaway car.

"Are you okay?" Her hand rested on his arm; it was strangely heavy for such a small woman.

He shrugged away from her touch and bent over at the waist, pinching his eyes closed against the fire searing down his calf. "I'll live."

Although the guys on his team would never let him live down losing a footrace to a thug, Ashley wasn't quite as likely to ride him about it. Then again, he'd lost a valuable opportunity to end this whole thing right there. Maybe she should rag on him for it.

He should have caught the guy. Should have finished this thing.

"I think he's gone." She took two small steps back, reaching her hand out to him again, more tentatively this time.

He shook his head with a wry grin and straightened all the way up.

"What's really going on with your leg?" In the dim streetlight, she glared at him. Hard. She meant business.

"Is that the look you give the kids here when they mis-behave?"

"Yes." She pulled on his arm until he stopped on the sidewalk leading to the front door. "I check out everyone who comes into this house, and you're no exception. You don't have to tell me the country, the mission or anything else classified. Just tell me what's wrong."

"I told you already—just a couple stitches near my knee."

Her pale fingers squeezed his biceps like a kitten bite. "How many is a couple? Do you need to see a doctor?"

He looked toward the clouds covering the moon. How much could he say without scaring her? This wasn't just about him. She had to worry about Tristan when he was deployed, too. She wouldn't just dismiss the injury. She couldn't. Not after ten years with a SEAL for a brother.

"About ninety."

Her mouth dropped open, and her grip weakened for a moment. Then she quickly shook her head. "How'd you get them?"

"A guy with a knife who wasn't very happy that I was trying to get us to the extraction point."

"Who is 'us'?"

He chuckled. "You know I can't tell you that."

She nibbled on her lower lip, staring at the ground for what felt like an hour. "Are you going to have to retire?"

He scooped her chin up with one finger; her skin was softer than suede. Her gaze darted around the street, around his arm, over his shoulder. Anywhere but his eyes. And it was suddenly clear. She worried about him. Not quite like she worried about Tristan. Not to the same extent, certainly. But she was concerned about his welfare, about his future.

He couldn't remember the last time someone had been really concerned about him. Sure, the other SEALs watched his back, and if he was in danger he knew that any one of them would dive into the line of fire for him, but they weren't so great at expressing concern—or any emotions at all. A punch in the arm was about as close as any of them got to saying "Hope you're okay" or "Get well soon." And aside from them, who else even gave him a second thought? His commanding officer was always yelling at him to be careful with C-4. His landlord was afraid he wouldn't make it back from a mission and would miss a rent payment.

But genuine concern for him as a whole? Maybe his social worker from way back when, Miss Jorgens. She had looked like she was going to cry when she dropped him off with the Wellseys nearly thirty years before. Maybe she'd known then about his foster dad's temper. It hadn't stopped her from driving away.

Well, it was only fair that Ashley worried about him. He was going to worry about her, too, until whoever was harassing her was caught.

"Someday I'll have to retire. But not this week. And certainly not because of this." He dismissed his leg with a flip of his hand.

Her breath came out slowly between tight lips. "Do you need to see a doctor? Should I take you to the hospital? Or back to your hotel?"

He snorted. "Do you know the ribbing I'd get from Tristan and the others if I let you drive me to a hospital? I could be gushing blood, and I still wouldn't let you do it."

Her gaze shot to his, humor completely gone. "Are you bleeding?"

The air around them filled with his laughter. "No." When the lines on her face disappeared and her shoulders relaxed, he winked. "I'm just slow and out of shape and apparently unable to dodge a car."

She gave him a half smile for his half joke. Sure, he wasn't in peak condition, but even with the leg, he could take most men. He just needed a little rehab. But he needed to work on that while he was in town.

"I'll be back to normal in no time."

When she was convinced of his general health, her eyebrows knitted together. "What about the guy that was here? Did you see his face? Or what kind of car he got into?"

"No." He slapped his hand against his thigh. It'd been dark, the man mostly in shadows, and all he'd seen of the car were blinding high beams. "But maybe you should call Chief Donal and let him know you had a prowler."

"I will." She glanced over her shoulder at the front door. "Will we see you tomorrow?"

And tonight, if you look out your window. There was no way he was going back to the hotel when there was any chance that the guy from earlier might come back. But he had a feeling Ashley wouldn't like that answer, so he kept it to himself for now. "I'll pick up what we need to fix those locks and be here first thing."

She sauntered to the front door, but turned back when he said, "Lock your door. Okay?"

She wrinkled her nose and shook her head. "It's like you don't know me at all." She offered a tiny wave before slipping inside.

He waited at the edge of the sidewalk for fifteen minutes, absently rubbing his leg, as the lights in the house turned out one by one. When all was dark, he strolled around the perimeter. No cigarette butts or footprints. Toys in the backyard clean and put away. The bushes hadn't been trampled. No sign of anyone lurking in the area.

That didn't mean their visitor wouldn't be back.

So Matt settled into his truck, stretched his legs across the bench seat and leaned against the passenger door. Crossing his arms, he watched.

Ashley rubbed her eyes and covered a yawn as she opened the front door.

Matt's hand, in midknock, dropped to his side. With his other hand, he held a brown paper bag out to her.

"New locks?"

"Muffins."

She laughed as she grabbed the bag and poked her head inside. More than a dozen in different varieties; the scent of cinnamon and brown sugar rose on waves of warmth. "Thank you. I was just making an omelet. These will go great with that."

Leading him into the hallway and over multicolored braided rugs toward the kitchen, she stole another sniff into the sack of fresh pastries.

The faces around the kitchen table looked up from coloring books and crayons with a mixture of surprise and concern. But their uncertainty disappeared as soon as they recognized Matt.

"Good morning." He nodded at Benita from the doorway, as though asking permission to enter, and when she smiled at him, he stepped into the room, still leaning on the edge of the doorframe.

"You all remember my friend Matt Waterstone, right?" She set the bag on the counter, then got back to work on the omelet. She poured the beaten eggs into a skillet on the stove and added ham and cheese as she introduced the others. "Matt, you met Benita and Julio and the girls last night. And this is Meghan, Greta and Sara's mom. She works the night shift at the hospital and just got in this morning."

Matt offered them a wide smile, somehow making himself shorter, less intimidating. Apparently he didn't take their welcome for granted, so he'd keep earning their trust. His broad shoulders couldn't be helped, but he wasn't so meaty as to look like a thug. In fact, he looked almost the opposite of the guy he'd chased away the night before.

The skin at the corners of his blue eyes wrinkled with his grin. How on earth did he look so refreshed? She'd lain awake for hours last night, listening for any sound out of the ordinary. And all she had to show for it were puffy eyes and a thundering headache.

"Very nice to meet you, Meghan." Matt stepped into the room just far enough to offer a handshake to the middle-aged woman. "Your daughters and I played a board game last night, and I'm sorry to report that I lost miserably. You have smart kids."

Meghan beamed at him but didn't say anything.

Matt relaxed back into his spot in the doorway, putting his hands in his jean pockets, his elbows loosely bent at his sides. The dark brown of his long-sleeve T-shirt made his hair look even lighter than usual; several curls fell over his forehead. He tossed his head, sending his curls back into place as he watched the kids, who had returned to their coloring.

She hadn't looked at any man more than just in passing since Paul, so why did Matt make her heart stutter?

When he caught her eye, he quirked the corner of his mouth and winked. She jumped, nearly sending the omelet onto the floor.

"What's wrong, Miss Ashley?" Julio ran up to her, his little eyes squinting, two lines appearing between his brows. "You're all red in the face."

Of course she was red in the face. She'd just been caught staring at a man she had no business looking at. Avoiding Matt's gaze at all cost, she offered a distraction. "Matt brought us muffins for breakfast. Who wants one?"

"Me!" Julio grabbed for the bag.

"Uh-uh, mister." She shook her head. "The table needs to be cleared and set first. And would someone please call Carmen and the others?"

When all was ready and everyone had assembled, they squeezed around the long wooden table. Ashley told herself that she sat next to Matt so that he wouldn't end up next to someone he might make uncomfortable, but that wasn't the entire truth.

His elbow bumped hers as he shoveled eggs into his mouth, and he whispered an apology, followed by surprising words of praise. "You're doing a good thing here."

The affirmation sent an unexpected burst of warmth straight through her chest, curling around her heart and leaving her a little bit breathless. She was doing something important.

But then why was someone threatening her?

With the breakfast dishes done and the kids doing crafts

at the table, she followed Matt into the rooms in need of window-lock repairs.

As he unscrewed a broken bolt, he handed her the warped hardware. "So do you want to talk about the girl you mentioned yesterday? Joy, right? Still think the threats are about her?"

Ashley glanced over her shoulder, peeking down the hall to make sure no one was close enough to hear them. She still whispered for good measure. "I can't be sure, since the notes never mention her by name. But I just don't see how it could be anyone else."

"Tell me more about the woman who brought her here." His attention moved from the screwdriver in his hand to land heavily on her face.

"Miranda. She lives on the other side of town and works in human resources at the tire plant."

"The same one that's been having layoffs?"

"Yes. Some of the women who work there have come to her when their husbands lose control. She always directs the women to me, and, if they want it, I do whatever I can to get them the help they need." A ball thumped against the opposite side of the wall that she leaned against, and she gave it three sharp raps.

"Sorry, Miss Ashley."

"Take it to the back patio, Julio. But put on a coat before you go outside."

After several seconds, the screen door slammed, and she continued, "Last week Miranda brought this girl— Joy—to the back door, which was strange."

"How so?"

"Miranda will tell anyone who wants to know about this place, but she's never brought women by in person. She always said it would put her in a sticky situation between the employees she was supposed to serve and their spouses. Some of the women work at the plant alongside their husbands. Miranda didn't want to get mixed up in domestic disputes that would spill into the workplace, but she couldn't just sit back and watch when one of the guys took his temper out on his wife. My guess is that Jimmy is pretty—"

"Jimmy?"

"Swift. You met him at the police station yesterday."

Matt nodded slowly, not like it took him more than an instant to remember the guy. More like he was trying to wipe away an unpleasant memory.

"Anyway, I think Jimmy pretty much sides with the guys in a dispute. As far as I'm aware, he's never spoken to Miranda about her work with us. But I got the feeling from Miranda that he knows about it and doesn't exactly approve, even though he's never tried to stop it."

"So if Miranda brought her in personally, then that means that Joy wasn't a wife or girlfriend or daughter to one of Swift's workers?"

Ashley chewed on her lower lip, rubbing a hand down the leg of her jeans. How much of her memories of that night were accurate? How much was conjecture? It had been so late when Miranda knocked on the door.

But it was their only lead and the only place for them to start.

"I don't think so. Miranda introduced the girl as Joy. And, like I said, she wouldn't say much more than her name."

"So you just took Miranda's word for it that…what? Joy was in trouble?"

"I didn't have to take anyone's word for it—her injuries spoke for themselves. She had bruises on each arm from her wrists to her elbows…and those were just the injuries I could see when she was fully dressed."

Joy really hadn't communicated beyond a few short statements. But the hope in her eyes when Ashley had asked if she needed a safe place to stay had spoken volumes.

Ashley had stayed calm and collected at the time, but thinking back now on that first encounter with Joy, she felt a shiver run along her spine. In all likelihood, the man who had caused those bruises was the man threatening her now. If he'd been that rough with Joy *before* she'd gotten away from him, Ashley shuddered to think what he might do to the girl if she was ever in his power again. No matter what, Ashley had to make sure that didn't happen.

She jumped, pulled from her thoughts as Matt strolled past her, into the hallway and toward Lil's room—the next room with a broken lock. Next to the laundry room, this was the smallest in the home. The single bed covered with a blue quilt looked even smaller than usual as Matt filled the space.

"As I was saying," Ashley continued, "Miranda said she didn't know much about Joy's situation except that she needed a place to go. Somewhere out of town. I have contacts at shelters in counties around the state, so I was able to get Joy set up at one of them."

"What did *Joy* say?"

"Aside from her name and age? Not much. Well, she nodded when I said I could set her up at a place out of town. Normally, if someone feels they need to leave town, I prefer to send them to stay with someone they already know. But she wouldn't give me the name of her parents or a relative, so I had nowhere else to send her." Ashley wrung her hands, reliving that night in her mind, second-guessing every decision she'd made to protect the girl. "Miranda seemed certain that she wasn't safe here in town. That whoever was abusing her would find her if she didn't get out of the county. I wasn't going to leave her unprotected. She's in a safe place now."

Matt finished installing the lock and turned to face her. She took a deep breath as his frown deepened and the grooves at the corners of his mouth grew. His eyes bore all the way through her as he crossed his arms over his chest. In response, her back straightened and she tilted her chin up. Maybe her choices with Joy hadn't been by the book—since she suspected the girl was underage, protocol said she should have contacted the police—but she stood by her decision.

He could fight her all day if he wanted. She wasn't going to back down, no matter what questions he asked. She'd done what she had to in order to protect the girl.

If he didn't like her answers? Well, he didn't have to stick around.

She could protect the women and children living at Lil's on her own.

An image of the shadowy figure lurking on her lawn the night before sent her stomach to the floor. What if she had another visitor and Matt wasn't there to scare him off?

It didn't do anyone any good to go over worst-case scenarios. She could do this. Paul had taught her that, after all. She was stronger than he'd ever given her credit for. She was stronger than Matt seemed to think, too.

"So Joy arrived right before you were almost run over and got that first note?"

Fists clenched at her sides, she started to defend herself. "I did the right..." His words sank in. "You're not upset that I didn't get more information about her before finding another place for her?"

He crossed the room in three steps, his stride swallowing the distance and invading her space in an instant. The intensity of his gaze left her struggling for air. He rested a hand on her shoulder and leaned in even closer.

Her breath released in a rush as she stumbled over the leg of Lil's bedside table, but his grip on her arm caught her before she fell.

The force of his gaze didn't lift, but at the last minute the corners of his eyes crinkled with a hint of a smile that never found its way to his mouth. "I'm so proud of you. Tristan talks about you all the time. He says you're amazing and that you're doing incredible things for the women here. He wasn't kidding."

Despite the blaze in her cheeks, she rolled her eyes as she searched for somewhere—anywhere—else to look. The spot where he still held her arm tingled like the buzz after a particularly sweet cupcake, and she slipped it out of his grasp, wrapping it around her stomach.

Whether the tingle originated from his touch or his kind words, she had no business feeling this way for any guy, let alone Matt Waterstone. Paul had made her tingle, too, at first, and she wasn't about to go there again. That beast was laid to rest, and she was just fine on her own. She didn't need any distractions from the women who needed her at Lil's.

He dropped his hand to his side and stepped back, and she stole a full breath.

"Well, that's the last of the broken locks. I'll have to go to a different store to find a new chain for the front door. So we're done for now." He tossed an old lock in the air and caught it without even looking at it. "What's next?"

She chewed on her bottom lip and shook her head. He had a plan. It was spelled out across his face in perfect penmanship. So why wasn't he in a rush to put it into action?

"I suppose we better find out who might be after Joy." The floorboards creaked as he shifted his weight to the other leg, flinched and shifted right back. "Where do you want to start?"

"I'll call the director at the home where Joy is staying right now to see if she's said anything about who hurt her. Our only other option is finding out if Miranda can tell us anything else."

"You think she wasn't completely honest with you when she dropped off Joy?"

"There's only one way to know for sure."

FIVE

"Do you think Miranda will be able to help us?"

Ashley twisted the edge of her shirt in her hands as Matt guided his truck toward Miranda's house. Several dark clouds drifted in front of the morning sun, making the few road signs this far out of town difficult to read. The overcast skies threatened rain but never quite followed through.

If only she knew for sure if Miranda had been entirely honest about what she knew when it came to Joy. This whole situation had been strange from the beginning, but that didn't mean that Miranda was mixed up in something. There were so many other factors to consider. Ashley wanted answers, but she didn't want to bring trouble to Miranda's doorstep if she wasn't involved.

"I just don't know." She rubbed her temple with two fingers; tension was already making her head throb. "I mean, yes, she's been strange lately. But that could be from any number of factors."

"Like what?" He didn't take his eyes off the road, but somehow she could still feel the touch of his gaze.

She shook her head. Miranda's struggles weren't exactly hers to share, but how could Matt help her find the creep making her life miserable if she didn't trust him with what she knew? She'd spent her entire adult life helping people make it through the worst kind of secrets. But they had to share those secrets before she could help. Maybe that was the case now, too.

The large, two-story farmhouse that loomed ahead let her off the hook.

"That's Miranda's place. Turn down the drive there." She pointed at the mailbox, which barely hung on to the wooden stand with rusted bolts, and Matt followed her motion. His truck lurched over the driveway in dire need of repair, and she bounced so hard that her hair brushed the once felt-covered ceiling.

"Sorry about that." As he slowed the truck to a crawl, he reached out to smooth down her hair. His hand brushed from the top of her head to her ear, a subtle grin accompanying his movement. She couldn't be sure if the pitch of her stomach was caused by his grin, the pressure of his touch or the pothole that sent her sailing into the passenger door.

He snatched his hand back to the steering wheel and cleared his throat. "Old truck, old shocks."

His words did little to fill the silence. When they finally pulled up to the end of the drive, she grabbed the door handle with a damp grip, ready to be free. It didn't open, so she yanked on it again. Still nothing.

In response to her sidelong glance, he offered, "It sticks sometimes." After telling her that he'd help her with it, he jumped from his seat and disappeared around the back of the truck. In less than a second, the door creaked open and Matt was holding out his hand to help her down.

Ignoring his hand, she lowered herself to the ground, her feet crunching the gravel as he swung the door closed. Mere inches between them, his breath stirred the hair that he had smoothed just moments before, and she sucked in a breath, holding it as she looked up into his face. He leaned in even closer, his head tilted toward her but never quite touching her. Pesky butterflies took a second spin around her insides, and she pressed both hands to her stomach.

Was he going to kiss her? Did she want him to?

"Ashley? What are you doing here?"

At Miranda's question Matt shot back about three feet, and Ashley slid toward the front of the truck to greet her friend.

"I'm so glad that you're home." She blinked several times, trying to focus on the questions she was there to ask.

Miranda's smile didn't reach her eyes as she tugged off mud-caked gloves and brushed grass blades from the knees of her jeans without ever taking her eyes off Matt. "I was just working in the garden." She nodded toward the shoulder-high cornstalks to her left. "You're a long way from Lil's."

"Yes, well…" Her tongue stuck to the roof of her mouth. She hadn't thought of a good excuse for coming for a visit. In more than two years of friendship, she could count on one hand the number of times she'd been to Miranda's house. Those had been social functions. Her daughter's graduation party. A retirement party for a mutual friend.

Now she had no valid reason for showing up unannounced.

With a SEAL, no less.

No valid reason except the truth. But if she jumped in before testing the waters, she could scare off Miranda, who happened to be their only lead.

She glanced at Matt out of the corner of her eye, the remnants of her butterflies another uninvited guest at this shindig. He lifted one eyebrow, as if asking if she wanted him to step in. She could offer only a quick shake of her head before turning back to Miranda.

"Well, actually… You see…"

Matt stepped forward then, his hand extended and

a bright smile on his face. "Ma'am." He nodded at the middle-aged woman, who immediately began running her fingers through her shoulder-length brown tresses. "I'm Matt Waterstone. Just came up from San Diego to visit Ashley this week."

"Good to meet you." She snatched her hand back as soon as she shook his, clutching her sodden gloves to her stomach as her eyes shifted back and forth between the two of them. "What's going on?"

"We came to speak with you about a girl named Joy."

Miranda's mouth dropped open, then pinched closed. She took two quick steps and crossed her arms over her chest as her eyebrows drew tightly together to form a single line across her forehead.

Just perfect. He'd scared her. What if Miranda completely shut down now?

She had to smooth the ripples out. Fast.

But before she could speak, he continued, despite Miranda's obvious reaction. "I understand that you've been a good friend to many women in this town."

Miranda glanced toward her garden before looking back at him. "I've tried to be, but what does that have to do with Joy?"

"We think Joy may be in some trouble."

Miranda's features pinched even tighter. "I don't understand what that has to do with me. Like I told Ashley when I dropped Joy off, I don't know anything about her really. She just needed a safe place to stay for a while and someone to help her get on her feet."

Miranda's search for an escape route intensified, so Ashley slid forward until she could reach the other woman's arm with a comforting touch that might just keep her grounded.

"Is there anything else that you remember about Joy?

Did she say anything to you about where she's from or how she got those bruises?"

Miranda continued staring at the ground, refusing to look up even when she answered. "Like I told you then, Joy found me in the office at the plant. She said one of the other women had told her I could get her help. End of story."

"And did she say who recommended you?"

Matt's question caught Miranda off guard, and she studied the gloves in her hands, looking for an answer that wasn't there. "I can't remember. No, I don't think she did."

A muscle in Ashley's back jumped, pulling her from Miranda's story. "You said she found you in the office. Did she work at the plant? Had you ever seen her before?"

Now Miranda met her gaze as she twisted the pink gloves beyond recognition. "Look, I want to help you, but I really don't have time to answer all of your questions. I have to get to work."

Matt relaxed his stance, suddenly appearing more like a casual San Diego surfer than a highly trained warrior. The muscles beneath his loose jacket were less intimidating with his hands tucked in the pockets of his cargo pants. "Do you usually have to work on Saturdays?"

"Sometimes."

He nodded, a knowing grin spreading across his face. "I know what you mean. I'm on duty some Saturdays, too." The way he said it, Ashley pictured him sitting behind the counter of a convenience store, reading a magazine during a slow afternoon shift. Miranda probably thought the same thing.

"I guess we all do what we have to so we can take care of our families."

Matt's whole body swayed as he nodded. "Do you have kids, Miranda?"

"A daughter in college."

"I bet that's not cheap."

A flicker of a smile crossed her face and disappeared before Miranda responded; the wall she'd held in place since their arrival was beginning to tip. "It's not. And I can't afford to lose my job at the plant."

Matt rubbed his chin, his fingers rasping over stubble. "I heard the plant is having a hard time. Chief Donal—" Miranda wrinkled her nose "—said it's been a rough year."

Had Miranda and the chief had a falling-out? He'd been a friend of her ex-husband, and Miranda and Donal had been linked socially once or twice in the last few years. She didn't seem too pleased with him now though.

"That's no secret. A third of the county has been laid off in the last eighteen months. So when my boss tells me to be in on Saturday, that's where I'll be."

"Sounds fair enough."

"Have a good weekend." With a curt nod Miranda stalked toward her home and stomped up the steps.

"You get the feeling she's not telling us everything she knows?"

Ashley pressed her hands to her hips and heaved a sigh that could have carried all the way into the house. "I'm not sure how much she knows, but I'm sure she was lying to us. There's no way Joy could have gotten into the office at the plant if she didn't work there. One of the women who stayed with us last year worked at the plant and I went with her to pick up some paperwork for a position transfer. I wasn't allowed past the front door."

"And?"

"And I can't believe I didn't realize it when she dropped Joy off. I must have been so consumed with getting Joy taken care of. I didn't ask very many questions. But I think she was making up that story."

The corner of his mouth rose in a lopsided grin that was

becoming more and more familiar. "Pretty smart, Sawyer." His right eyelid twitched when he said her name, but there wasn't time to dwell on that. Or the way he'd leaned in to maybe almost kiss her earlier that morning.

First, they had to figure out their next step now that they knew Miranda wouldn't or couldn't share anything more about Joy. Her forearms burst out in goose bumps. The weight of someone watching her was almost tangible.

She twisted and turned, searching for any glimpse of someone hiding in the bushes or around a tree, but there was no one else in the yard—at least, no one she could see.

Matt frowned and spun around just like she had. "What's wrong?"

"Nothing. It just felt like..." She was just being paranoid. There was no one here. "Never mind. Let's go."

He tugged on the passenger door of his truck until it popped and motioned for her to climb in. Just as she grasped the seat to hoist herself into the cab, a slamming door made her jump back to the ground.

"Wait!" Miranda scurried toward them, brushing dirt off her gardening jeans as she arrived. Matt's face didn't change, but his posture turned to steel, every nerve on full-alert. But Miranda didn't notice. She wasn't looking at him. "Did anything happen to Joy? I mean, is she still safe?"

Ashley squeezed the other woman's upper arm. "I'm sure she's fine. I won't let anything happen to her. I promise."

"But she's not here, right? She's not in Charity Way?"

Matt shook his head so subtly that she almost missed it. He was right. She couldn't tell anyone, let alone someone who wasn't telling all her secrets, where Joy had been placed. If the notes were really because of Joy, then it stood to reason that they might affect Miranda, too. Someone who thought of Joy as his property would use any means necessary to get at her.

Maybe even forcing Miranda to tell what she knew.

It was better for everyone if she didn't know that Joy had moved into a long-term house two counties over.

"She's safe. We'll protect her."

The *we* popped out before she even thought about it. When had she started thinking about Matt as her partner in all this? It was fine to have him around. He was handy with the security at the house, and he seemed concerned about her welfare. But partnership had never been something she'd intended to offer.

She'd fought to protect the women at Lil's by herself for years. Lil was more den mother than mother bear. More listening ear than bared teeth. Ashley was the one who stood up for the shelter and its residents.

The threats. The angry, midnight calls from abusers. The graffiti on her home. The sneers from local business owners more interested in appearances than grace.

She'd dealt with them all on her own. And she'd deal with them on her own when Matt went back to San Diego. No point in thinking they were a long-term team.

Best just to be thankful for his help on this case and prepare to handle the next alone.

No problem.

Miranda's sigh seemed to come from her entire body, her shoulders relaxing and chin falling in one motion. Her hand slipped into her pocket, and she bent her elbow out from her body. "I wish I could give you something, anything, to help Joy."

"It's all right if you don't know anything." Ashley bit her lip.

Miranda kept her gaze trained on her once-white sneakers and shook her head. "I can't tell you anything." Suddenly her gaze shot up, her eyes filled with the same gray storm clouds as the sky. "I have to go to work. I'm sorry I can't say more."

She dashed back toward the house as though a starting pistol had fired.

Ashley hung her head. "Why can't she say more? She obviously cares about Joy. Why won't she just tell us who's looking for her?"

Matt stooped in front of her, then rose with an outstretched hand. "She dropped this. I don't think it was an accident."

She snatched the white scrap of paper from between his fingers, turning it over and over. It was thicker than regular paper, but not quite cardboard, with bent corners and a frayed edge along one of the shorter sides.

"Part of a matchbook?" Matt suggested.

"I think so." She flipped it over again for good measure. "I can't remember the last time I saw one of these."

"What is Miranda not saying with this?" Matt took his turn analyzing the scrap. "And what's this gold logo?" His callused finger traced the embossed infinity sign on the front.

"I know where that is."

Matt placed his arm on the back of the bench seat to look over his shoulder as he backed out of Miranda's driveway. "So what exactly is this place?"

"It was a bar." He raised an eyebrow at Ashley, who shrugged. "There was a woman staying at Lil's more than a year ago, and her ex-boyfriend worked there as a bouncer. It's about three blocks from your hotel."

As she turned to face him, her shoulder brushed his fingers, and his breath caught for an instant. Just like it had when he'd helped her down from the truck. When he'd stood close enough to smell her citrus shampoo. When he'd leaned toward her just to feel connected.

When he'd nearly kissed her.

Just before he remembered that she was Tristan's kid sister.

What had he been thinking?

He hadn't been. A complete and utter lapse in brain activity was the only explanation for letting her smile twist his gut like that.

Hadn't Tristan told him time and again that no guy was good enough for Ashley? Especially a guy like Matt, with his string of foster fathers who had taught him plenty about fighting back and fighting hard, but nothing about relationships without bad tempers and heavy fists. No, Tristan would hit the roof if he knew Matt felt anything more than protective instincts for Ashley. Hadn't he said that he'd shoot first and ask questions later if a man even looked at her with anything less than respect?

But a lack of respect wasn't really the problem here. He'd never met a woman he respected more than Ashley. What she did with the women at Lil's was nothing short of incredible. The way she dealt with thugs and losers put his first foster mothers to shame. He'd known only three other women in his life that served others with such grace and grit—his pastor's wife, his last foster mom and Mrs. Sawyer.

That was probably where Ashley learned it.

None of this meant he needed to act on any impulses. Especially those that involved kissing her.

"Turn right here." Ashley had turned away from him as he drove through town, her features growing tighter as they passed dilapidated buildings with neon signs and taped-up windows. "It's at the end of the next block, up there."

The very last building on the right looked like it should

have been condemned. The gray, shuttered walls bowed like a grenade had exploded inside, and the roof sagged along the ridgepole from end to end. Weeds had taken up residence around the front door, obscuring the already tenuous wooden steps.

But the infinity symbol above the door clearly marked this as their target.

"Was it like this when it was open?"

Ashley twisted to look up at the tattered shingles as she worried on her bottom lip. "I don't think so."

"Maybe you should stay in the truck." He pulled up to the curb, eyeing the two men drinking from brown paper bags outside the store next door. "I'll just duck inside the Infinity, and you can stay in here. With the doors locked."

"Not likely."

He chuckled as he stepped out of his car. Ashley was on his heels in a moment. She didn't touch him, but he could feel her body heat on his back through his jacket. If she insisted on joining him, at least she had the good sense to stick close.

He offered her a hand as they approached the steps, and she clung to his forearm when she wobbled on a loose board.

"It's not too late to go back to the truck."

"I'm just fine." Her wrinkled nose and pursed lips weren't in agreement with her words, but she refused to leave his side.

The front door handle jiggled but stuck and refused to give in when he applied pressure. "Somebody wants you to think he doesn't give a rip about this place, but that lock is solid."

"Can you break it down?"

"What do you think I am?"

"Well, excuse me." She pulled her hand away from his

and glowered up at him. She looked tough, but she couldn't keep her smirk at bay for long. "I thought you were strong enough."

"Oh, I can break the door in. I'm just not going to."

"You're not?"

"I'm okay with entering. Just not with breaking and entering." Taking caution to avoid the rotted boards on his way down to the curb, he reached out to help her again. This time, instead of taking his arm, she slipped her hand into his. Soft like a flower and warm like sun-drenched sand, it was a perfect fit.

She pulled away as soon as they reached the sidewalk, and he forced himself to focus his thoughts on what might be inside the old bar that Miranda wanted them to see.

He led her through the knee-high grass around the corner of the building and onto another nearly deserted street. All of the buildings along the road seemed to have been forgotten, and there wasn't a car parked in any of the gravel lots or shrub-filled alleys except for a rusted-out old Buick up on blocks. Signs identifying the businesses had vanished a long time before.

"How long ago did this bar close?"

"Maybe a year?"

He kicked a piece of wood paneling that had fallen from the wall. "It must have been in bad shape even when it was open."

Ashley shrugged. "This isn't exactly the best neighborhood."

That was a serious understatement.

A small window at the back of the building probably led to what had been a second-story stockroom, or maybe an employee break room. After all, bars weren't known for their natural light in the main areas. At fourteen, he'd dragged his foster dad out of more than one seedy club, and they all had the same thing in common: neon lights and no windows. But when he'd sneak in through the alley doors, he'd often see employees catching fresh air through the break room's open window.

Maybe that's how this one had been used.

The bottom of the window frame was at least three feet above his head, and he looked around the ground for something to stand on. "Do you see a cinder block or piece of wood around here? I just need a little lift and I'll be able to get to the window."

"Nope. But I'll do it."

His eyebrows pinched together, despite her innocent smile. "You'll do what?"

"Just give me a boost. I'll see if it's open, and if it is, I'll run around and unlock the back door."

"I'm not sending you in alone before we know who or what's in there." He pointed a single finger at the other buildings on the street. "You have no idea who could have taken over this property. Anyway, this is all tied to Joy, which is the reason that someone tried to run you over." His last word ended in a growl, and she jumped.

Pressing her hands to her hips, she leaned forward like she was talking to a kid. Except she had to tilt her head all the way back to look right into his eyes. "You don't have to remind me. I know Joy's in trouble—"

"You, too."

"—and we're here to figure out why. Let's find what Miranda couldn't tell us. We don't have time to waste arguing."

He began to spit back a definitive no, but he stopped short. She was right.

And he hated it.

The driver of the car, the author of the notes and their

late-night visitor would be back. They had to figure out who he was before he returned. And this was their only lead.

"Tell you what." Ashley's voice had never risen, but her tone turned firm, and it was clear that she expected no argument. "If you'll give me a boost, I'll look around inside. If there's anything that looks like someone might have moved in, we'll find another way in. I'll be careful. I promise."

He shook his head as he crossed his fingers and bent over to let her step into the cradle. Her fingernails pinched into his shoulders as he cupped her shoe and slowly stood. "You okay?"

"Just fine. Can you get me closer to the wall?"

He stepped toward the building as she walked her hands up the siding. The top of her head just reached the bottom of the glass. She gave it a shove, but nothing happened.

"Can you get me a little higher?" When he boosted her to his shoulder level, she pushed on the glass again, and it creaked open about three inches. She ducked to peer through the opening. "Empty shelves. Dust everywhere, even on the floor. No one's been walking through here anytime in the last several months."

The window groaned as she lifted it open farther. "I'm going in."

SIX

Matt knew he should go around to the back door to meet her, but he couldn't walk away until he knew she was safe in the room. If she screamed or called out for him, then he'd find a way to get to her.

As he paced the width of the window, Ashley shrieked, just seconds after landing in the room. She sounded more startled than scared, but it was more than enough to galvanize him into action. Without another thought, he flew at the open window.

Matt cracked the window frame when his elbow slammed against it, but he didn't feel a thing as he wedged through the narrow opening. Instinct and years of training took over as he curled into a ball and rolled across the floor.

As he spun, he made out Ashley's form to his left, sitting on the floor and backed up against the battered shelves. Her knees were tucked up nearly to her chin. Eyes bigger and bluer than ever as she trembled.

Taking his gaze off her for a moment, he scanned the rest of the room. The rest of the empty room.

"What…" he started to ask, his voice trailing off.

"That," Ashley answered.

He followed the line of her finger to the wall next to

the door and saw a rat that looked like it would be more at home in the New York City sewer system than little Charity Way. Its ears turned toward them as its hind end swayed back and forth on squat legs.

Matt pushed himself to his full height and stabbed his fingers through his hair. "You screamed because of a mouse?"

"That is not a mouse. It's the size of a Volkswagen." She scooted farther away, trying to disappear into the shelves.

The rat shot toward a hole under one of the shelves, and Matt let it go, certain that Ashley would breathe easier once it was out of sight. "Why are you on the floor?"

"It scared me, and I fell backward."

He squatted down in front of her, thankful that his elbow stung more than his leg for the moment. "Did you hurt yourself?"

"No." Her breathing seemed easier, her shoulders rising and falling in quick succession. "I'm all right. Just startled me."

"Then we're even." He grabbed her hands and pulled her to her feet right beside him. When he'd slapped the dust off her black sweater, he wrapped an arm around her shoulders and tugged her into his side. Her heart raced against him, matching the jarring rhythm of his own.

There couldn't be anything wrong with this, could there?

He was just offering her an older-brother-type hug, just trying to calm her down.

Not at all focusing on the way her arm snaked around his waist or her head rested against his shoulder.

"Thank you." She sighed before putting two feet between them, her features a mixture of confusion and anxiety. "I can handle anything but rats."

Putting another step between them, he tilted his head toward the door. "You ready to look around?"

She nodded and followed him to the door leading to the main bar room. He cracked it open but could see next to nothing in the almost complete darkness. "Stay on my six," he whispered as he stepped out next to the bar top that spanned the entire length of the room.

Refusing to break the silence—and keeping an eye out for any of the rat's friends—he slid a hand along the wall until he found the knob for the front door. As he'd suspected, the lock was new and sturdy, but it yielded easily enough from the inside. Once the door was open, there was enough light to pierce the darkness and illuminate the emptiness.

The wooden floorboards creaked with each step, matching the echo set off by each footfall.

"Do you see anything?"

Ashley squinted at him, still having a hard time seeing in the semidarkness. "What are we supposed to be looking for?"

"I don't suppose someone left a picture of Joy with his name and address on the back."

Without any furniture to hamper them, the search only took fifteen minutes.

And left them empty-handed.

"I don't know what I'm looking for." Ashley sighed as she spun in a slow circle. "There's nothing here except cobwebs and dust." She slapped her hands on the thighs of her jeans and looked at her palms like they belonged to someone else.

He knew the feeling. It was the same one growing in his gut. This was a dead end with echoing floorboards.

"Why would Miranda send us on a wild-goose chase?" Ashley walked into the storage room and unlocked the back door. The afternoon clouds were not able to stop the sunlight from sneaking all the way into the main room.

"I don't know. But she did." He followed the illuminated dust particles dancing in the breeze to Ashley's side. The steps that must have once led up to the door had disappeared, leaving only the wooden bases and a four-foot drop.

"Should we head back to the house?" She flipped her hand toward the street. "I want to make sure nothing's happened and call my contact at the house that Joy went to again. I haven't heard back from her yet."

"Is that unusual?"

She looked up at the sky and pressed her hands to her hips. "Not really. Some days I can be so busy that I don't even have time to eat, let alone check my messages. I'm sure she's the same way."

"All right. Let's go back."

"But there are no steps." Her eyebrows lifted. Her pursed lips asked the question behind her words.

"It's this or the rotted-through front entrance." He slipped past her and jumped to the ground. The ache in his injured leg wasn't much more than a twinge when he landed, so he smiled as he turned around and held out his arms.

She had other ideas. Pushing his hands to the side, she jumped on her own, her knees perfectly absorbing the impact. Where had she learned to do that?

Apparently she could read his mind. "Gymnastics until I was twelve."

"Why'd you give it up?"

"I couldn't handle the pressure of it all after my dad died."

He was such an idiot. Of course her dad died more

than twelve years before—he knew the whole story from Tristan. "I'm so sorry, Ash. I wasn't thinking."

"It's okay. Long time ago."

Her voice was steady, but her eyes focused on a point down the street instead of meeting his gaze.

It's just what he did. The minute he started getting close to any woman, he fumbled it. He just had so little experience with normal, healthy relationships between a man and a woman that he never quite knew what to say or do.

Tristan, on the other hand, had always had a way with the ladies, smooth and easy, he'd sweep them off their feet before they even knew he was there. Like a Chinook chopper flying under the radar, Tristan would swoop in.

He was pretty much the opposite.

Good thing he wasn't trying to get closer to Ashley.

Good thing he wasn't looking for any kind of relationship with anyone. He wasn't the marrying kind. There were just too many skeletons in his closet. Too many broken bones and beatings. Too many angry foster dads.

He wasn't going to let that define him. And he wasn't going to perpetuate it either.

"You folks looking to buy this place?"

Yanked back to the present by the old man's question, Matt bit down on his tongue as he appraised the man leaning against the liquor store next to the Infinity. "Just checking it out. Why do you ask?"

"It could use a new owner." Wrinkled hands shook as he lifted a brown paper bag to his face and sucked down whatever was inside. His nose shone like a fairytale reindeer; his eyes were watery and his skin paper-thin. He ran a hand over his white hair, apparently trying to bring some semblance of order to the greasy mess. "Nobody takes care of it."

"What do you mean?" Ashley leaned toward the man,

despite the stench radiating from him. The toothless grin and waggling eyebrows were directed at Ashley, and Matt cringed at the attempted flirtation. Ashley put her hand on the old man's shoulder and smiled at him.

"Just what I said. Some big shot bought the bar last year and then closed it up, like we were nothing. Where's a man to get a cold one when the only bar in this area closes up shop?" He frowned and took another swig. "It's just plain wrong is what it is."

If the twitch of Ashley's cheeks was any indication, she was having just as hard of a time as he was keeping a straight face in light of the man's irony. Did the stranger not realize that he held a bottle in his hand and leaned against a store that sold beer and any other type of alcohol?

Matt managed to get control of his humor first and prodded their informant. "Did you ever see this big shot?"

"Who?"

Ashley bit her lip and looked toward the clouds, which nearly sent him laughing, too. He swallowed a bubble of laughter and took a deep breath. "The man who bought this place."

The old man swore worse than some of the guys in the teams. "No way would he show his face in this neck of the woods. Too embarrassed, if you ask me. He knew he'd get a piece of our minds. Me and the other regulars. We'd have showed him what was what."

"Do you know what his name is? I mean, this isn't a very big town. You must have heard his name mentioned."

He swayed violently as he leaned away from the wall, scratching at the gray whiskers on his chin. "Nope." He pursed his lips, eyes only on Ashley. "But maybe you and me could go get some dinner."

"You think that would help you remember who bought this place?"

"Nope." He moved the brown bag in a circle over his stomach. "But I sure do like the comp'ny of a perty girl when I get some grub."

At this Ashley had to turn away, her face breaking and shoulders shaking with silent laughter. Matt couldn't look at her without joining in, so he kept his gaze on the old man. "I'm afraid we have other plans this evening. But is there anything else you can tell us about who might have bought this building?"

"Nope." He staggered back against the wall. The wrinkles on his forehead relaxed as though having the wall for support allowed him to think clearly. "Like I said, I never saw him—just the construction crews he sent."

"Construction crews?" Matt glanced dubiously back at the building. It looked like it hadn't received any kind of regular maintenance in way too long. If construction crews had been around, what had they done?

Below bushy eyebrows, brown eyes swept the still deserted street. "They brung in one of those earthmovers. Hauled out a bunch of dirt. Dug around for about a month or so."

"When was this?" Ashley had her game face back on.

"Right after it closed, I guess. Prob'ly around the same time I started coming here." He hitched a thumb over his shoulder.

"Do you live around here, Mr...." Her voice trailed off, waiting for him to fill in his name.

"Nope. 'Bout three blocks that way." He pointed his bag toward the Infinity. "But I'm here most every day since they laid me off."

This guy looked old enough to have been retired. Twice. "The tire plant?" Matt asked.

"Yup."

"I'm sorry to hear that." And he really was. "Thanks for answering our questions."

"You gonna buy this place?"

"Probably not today." Ashley slipped a business card from her back pocket and held it out to him. "But if you ever need a hot meal, you can call this number. A friend of mine delivers good meals every day."

His eyes narrowed at them, a wall of injured pride suddenly stemming the flow of information. "I don't need nobody's charity."

She winked at him as she tucked the card into the chest pocket of his trench coat. "Everyone in town has had some rough times. So just in case."

"You were pretty good with him."

Ashley latched her seat belt before offering Matt a smile. "I nearly lost it a few times. Was he really asking me on a date?"

"I'm pretty sure that's what he was thinking."

She chuckled again. "I couldn't believe it. He was ridiculous. For a few minutes out there, I forgot that there's a lunatic after one of my girls." Determination swept over his face like an eclipse, blocking the humor that had made him look ten years younger. She was sorry to see it go. It felt good to laugh with a man. Although Matt hadn't really laughed, had he? The amusement in his eyes had been louder than any belly laugh she'd ever heard from him. Actually, she'd never heard him all-out laugh. Strange that she'd never thought about it before.

"I wish you wouldn't say it like that."

"What?"

He turned the wheel toward her home and didn't take his eyes off the road as he responded. "You talk as though the guy who tried to run you over and showed up at your house a couple nights ago isn't after you personally."

"Well, he's not. Not really."

"But he's not going to just go around you. If Joy is who he really wants, then he'll go through you to get her. He has no other choice. No one else in town knows where she is."

Pain shot through her temples, and her chin fell to her chest. Why did he insist on reminding her? She wasn't ignorant about the threat. They'd talked about almost nothing else since he'd arrived.

It didn't mean they were any closer to figuring out who was behind it all.

His voice was low and throaty when he finally spoke again. "I don't mean to scare you. And I'll do everything in my power to protect you. I promised your brother I would." Over the rumbling engine of his truck, he let out a breath between tight lips. "I just want you to take this seriously."

"I do. I won't let anything happen to one of my girls—"

"Not for your girls. Take this seriously for yourself. You're the target here."

She turned to his silhouette, highlighted against the setting sun. "I know that."

He pulled his truck up to the curb in front of Lil's just as the sun disappeared for the night. Once he parked, he turned to look at her for the first time since getting back behind the wheel. "I know you want to take care of the families here, and I want that, too. But without you they're all at risk. So let's keep you safe."

They weren't particularly poignant words, but for some reason the back of her eyes began to sting, and she had to look back down at her hands clasped together between her knees.

People had said it before. Tristan had said it a hundred times. But for some reason when Matt said that her work was valuable, a band tightened around her chest. She wanted to be valuable. She wanted to help these women.

Mostly she wanted no woman to ever go through what she'd endured.

She unlocked the front door and let them both in. "Let me just check my messages to see if there's any word on Joy." Matt nodded as he wandered off toward the kitchen. She ducked into her study. Picking up her private line, she listened to the short message, which was from Cathy, the other house director. Ashley hadn't included any specifics when she'd called the other day, not wanting to spook the other woman, so she'd just asked Cathy to get back to her as soon as she could.

She punched in the number from memory.

"This is Cathy."

"Hi, it's Ashley."

The other woman had long ago passed retirement age, but her voice still rang with youthful joy. "Ashley, honey. How are you? Is everything all right?"

"Yes. Of course. I was calling to check on you and Joy."

"Oh, we're fit as fiddles."

"Has she said anything?" Ashley tapped her pen on her desk, aching for something, anything that would help them find answers.

Cathy's voice dropped to a whisper, and Ashley heard the sound of a door closing. "She hasn't said much of anything really. She just keeps asking if she has to go back."

"Back where?"

"She won't say. Just back to wherever she came from."

Ashley sighed, the band around her chest tightening again. What if she wasn't strong enough to protect Joy? She had to be. She just had to. "What did you tell her?"

"That she's safe and that she doesn't have to go anywhere."

"Thank you, Cathy. Will you let me know if there's any trouble?"

"Absolutely."

After hanging up, she took several deep breaths.

Joy was safe for now. And there wasn't any reason to worry Cathy yet. No one else knew where Joy had been stashed.

Her worries about Joy assuaged for a moment, Ashley walked to the kitchen and nearly burst out laughing for the second time that day.

Two little girls in pigtails sat around the table, heads bent intently over princess coloring books. Their crayons moved in precise motions, staying inside the lines. And Matt was in the middle of it all.

He hunched over his own page, the red marker in his hand setting a twirling skirt aflame.

"But her dress is supposed to be blue."

Matt turned to Greta on his right, his face a mask of confusion. "Supposed to be?"

Greta rolled her eyes and shook her head. "It's Cinderella, silly. She wears a blue dress. That's the one that her fairy godmother made her."

"Fairy godmother?"

"Haven't you ever seen the movie?"

Matt shook his head, his motions slow and serious. "Maybe you should tell me about it. What happens?"

Just as Greta launched into the story of the girl and her wicked stepmother, Matt glanced toward the doorway. A slow smile spread across his mouth, and he winked.

Greta never talked if she didn't have to, and there she was spilling every detail of the movie to a man at least three times her size. How had he done it? How could a highly trained warrior be gentle enough to befriend a spooked little girl? How'd he make her so at ease that she'd scrambled over every internal wall to tell him the tale of the little cinder girl?

Ashley didn't even feel that easy around him.

But that probably had more to do with unwanted butterflies and a near—and definitely unwanted—kiss.

"What's for dinner, Miss Ashley?" One of the other girls looked up from her Belle and Jasmine picture long enough to ask the important question of the evening.

"Well, Sara, I have no idea. Let's see what we have." In front of the open refrigerator, she called out their options. "We could make spaghetti. Or corn chowder. Or hot dogs and mac and cheese."

Sara scrunched up her face. "I hate hot dogs."

Matt leaned over and mock-whispered, "Me, too."

He winked at her again, and Ashley stuck her head back in the refrigerator. What was with all the winking? Had he developed a nervous tic since arriving in town?

Grabbing the stuff to make spaghetti, she dumped everything on the counter and pulled pots and pans from their cabinets. Managing to keep her back to the table to avoid any more errant winks, she worked on preparing dinner.

"Greta, will you please clear off the table? And the rest of you can set it."

Within seconds Matt stood by her side. "Point me to the plates."

Despite the winks and butterflies, it wasn't so bad having him around. In fact, he made it a little easier to breathe. If anyone came looking for Joy, he'd find more than six feet of SEAL instead.

But Matt would go back to the hotel tonight. After dinner. After the dishes were washed and put away. After everyone else had gone to bed.

She'd still be awake.

Listening. Waiting.

She stepped into the main entrance and called down the hallway. "Lil, Carmen! Dinner!"

And then her world exploded in a shower of broken glass.

SEVEN

As soon as he heard the crashing sound, Matt flew into action.

"Stay here. Don't move," he ordered his little friends as he ran toward the front of the house.

Even before he turned the corner into the main entry, the cold December wind whipped at his face. His feet pounded on the wooden floor as he rounded the turn.

"Ash. Ash, can you hear me?" Ignoring the crunch of glass beneath his knees as he knelt by her head, he searched his pocket for a handkerchief to stop the flow of blood trickling from the cut on her forehead. His pockets were empty, so he grabbed at the hem of his T-shirt sleeve and yanked. Ashley blinked at the same moment his shirt let out a high-pitched rip. He wadded up the cotton and pressed it against her wound.

"Are you all right?"

She kept one eye closed but let the other one gaze around the walls and ceiling, finally landing back on Matt's face. "I think so. My head hurts."

"It should. You got hit by a brick." He picked up the brick next to her head to show her, only then noticing the note taped to its side.

The words were scrawled in uneven swirls and smudged by some sort of liquid, but the message was loud and clear.

I want my property back, or you'll lose one of your precious girls.

"Goodness! What happened?" Lil's eyes swam with fear. Her bones creaked as she lowered herself to the floor at Ashley's side and reached for her blood-smeared cheek. "Honey, I'm here."

"Can you hold this to her head for a second?" The woman moved so slowly that Matt nearly picked up her gnarled hand and put it in place. "There. Hold it tight. I'll be right back."

Ashley grabbed the hem of his shirt and tugged twice. "Don't leave me." Her breath came in short gasps, matching his own accelerated rate. He wrapped his hand around her wrist, resting two fingers near the base of her palm, automatically checking her pulse.

"We had a visit from our friend. I'm just going to see if he's still around."

Confusion washed over her face but was quickly replaced by concern. She nodded against Lil's hand and let go of his shirt. "You'll be back?"

"In just a second."

Glass crunched as he sailed over it and out the front door, barely giving the broken window next to it a second look.

As he raced down the sidewalk, the truth punched him in the stomach. Every car on the block belonged to a neighbor. He'd seen the gray sedan, the blue coupe and the red speedster parked in the same spots two nights ago when he'd slept in his truck.

And just like two nights ago, he'd missed the lunatic.

But this time Ashley had been hurt, and the threatening note couldn't be construed as anything else.

Time to call Chief Donal.

He dug into his pocket for his cell phone and called the police station.

After being assured that an officer was on his way, Matt hurried back to Ashley's side. A small mob had congregated around her, each woman clucking and shushing and pushing her down every time she tried to stand up.

She looked up into the faces of the hovering women and tenderly pressed a finger to the little cut on her forehead. "I'm fine. Look. Hardly any blood."

A hitch in her voice propelled Matt through the crowd. He squeezed his way between the women and children, then he scooped Ashley into his arms. "Let's find a more comfortable place for her to sit." The faces surrounding them nodded, wide-eyed and fearful.

Holding in a sigh, he offered a gentle smile. "Ashley's going to be fine. The police are on their way here, but we should move into the living room so no one cuts themselves on the glass."

Every woman looked at her feet as if just realizing the sharp shards scattered across the floor could be dangerous. They herded the little ones toward the back of the house, Matt following behind.

Her weight in his arms felt good. There was something about the way she didn't bother to lift her head off his shoulder or loosen her grip around his neck—even when she said, "I can walk, you know."

"I know." He didn't set her down.

"Are you all right?"

He jerked at her question. "Of course. I didn't get hit by a brick."

"I meant because you didn't find anyone outside."

Oh. That.

Yes, that was going to bug him for a bit. How had he

let the jerk slip through his fingers twice? He just couldn't dwell on it so long that he missed his next chance.

"How'd you know I didn't find him?"

She pushed hair out of her face by rubbing her cheek against his shoulder and closed her eyes. "You'd still be out there if you had." Her long lashes fluttered, matching the shivers down his spine, but she didn't raise her baby blues in his direction. Instead she sighed and snuggled a little farther into his chest, nearly asleep as he bent over the couch to set her down.

Would she look that peaceful after he kissed her?

He took a deep breath to push aside the fleeting thought, but it backfired. Her citrus perfume smelled of clean dishes and the orange groves near his house in San Diego. She smelled like home. She would be a good fit in his home.

Except he had nothing to offer her. A meager senior chief's salary, a checkered past and a last name that came from a man he'd never met.

He needed to get it together. No more thoughts of oranges or lingering kisses.

Just focus on his promise to Tristan.

Tristan, who was on an op somewhere in the Middle East. Tristan, who had been his best friend for almost ten years. Tristan, who would never approve of Ashley dating a man with his history.

As he stepped back from the couch, Lil took over the situation. "Carmen, would you see about dinner, please? It's probably cold by now. Meghan, would you sweep up the glass in the entry? And, Julio, would you go get an ice pack for Miss Ashley's head?"

The two women and little boy took off without a word as Lil corralled the others toward the kitchen. "Mr. Waterstone, would you—"

Red and blue lights flashed through the bay window. "I'll go speak with the officers."

As Matt reached the sidewalk, Chief Donal wrenched himself from behind the steering wheel of the cruiser. "Waterstone, what are you doing here?"

"We were just about to have dinner when a brick came through the window next to the front door."

The older man glared, clearly not missing the fact that his first question hadn't been answered. "Was anyone injured?"

"It grazed Ashley's head and knocked her out, but she came to after just a few seconds and she says she's fine."

"Do I need to call the paramedics?"

"Why don't you come inside and see?"

The chief complied, strolling toward the house. "You see who threw it?"

"No. But they left another note."

"Another?"

Matt quirked an eyebrow at the older man. "I don't think it's a stretch to say that this was the same guy who left the last two notes."

The chief wrinkled his bulbous nose and crossed his arms. "We can't assume anything."

"How about we assume that there's no such thing as a coincidence?"

With one hand tucked into his armpit and the other scratching one of his chins, Donal nodded. "All right."

They walked into the house, Donal leading the way.

Matt stopped him with a heavy hand on his shoulder just inside the door and pointed to the evidence on the corner table. "I haven't shown this to Ashley yet. I doubt you'll be able to get any fingerprints off something so porous, but I just touched the edges here and here."

The chief bent over, bobbing his head closer to the red

block to make out the mangled words. "You're right about one thing, son."

"What's that?"

"There's no denying she's in trouble."

"And you're sure you didn't see anything?"

Ashley rubbed the tender bump on her head, answering the same question for the umpteenth time. "Yes. It was dark outside, and I could only see the reflection of the hallway light in the window. Plus, I wasn't really trying to see outside."

"Where were you looking?"

She bit her tongue to keep from telling him what a ridiculous question that was and took a deep breath before responding. "Just down the hall. I was calling everyone for dinner, and I was checking to see who was on their way."

The room suddenly seemed smaller, the air a little thinner. Matt stood in the doorway, carrying a hammer and a handful of nails.

She tried to smile at him, but the muscles in her face were frozen.

"All boarded up. We'll call the glass guy tomorrow. You okay in here?"

"Thank you." She nodded, and the chief stood, taking it as his invitation to leave.

"We'll do what we can to get prints off that brick, and I'll ask Bob to drive the neighborhood tonight, Miss Sawyer. But I can't make any promises."

She swallowed, taking several breaths before speaking. She couldn't have her voice cracking again. "Have you gotten anything off the other notes I brought in?" Before it had been notes and threats. Now some man had vandalized her property. What if it had been one of the other women hit? Or one of the kids?

They had to do something.

Soon.

He shook his head, and she inhaled against the tightness in her chest. "Please let us know if you find anything."

"I will. Try to have a good evening, and be sure to get over to the hospital if your headache gets worse."

She nodded as the chief walked out, Matt close behind. They kept their voices low, but she could still make out most of their conversation by the front door.

"I don't want to worry her," the chief said, "but we just don't have a big enough department to take on her personal protection."

Matt growled something that sounded an awful lot like "I'll handle it."

"Just be sure to call in the authorities if you run into any trouble." Matt cleared his throat, but Donal continued in a firm voice, "I know you're a man quite capable of handling this situation. But you have no authority here, so don't get in over your head."

Matt must have nodded, because the door opened and closed, the sound echoing in the strangely silent house. All of the kids were in their rooms, playing quietly, probably on threat of punishment from their moms.

But were they even safe there?

Her stomach clenched as she waited for Matt to return. He didn't. Instead he walked past the living room door toward the kitchen.

Tempted to relax and let him deal with the whole situation, she leaned into the high back of the couch. Her heart squeezed then thumped as she rolled the idea around in her mind. Matt had already stepped in time and again, what was the harm in letting him take charge now?

Except letting a man be strong for her never seemed to end well.

Paul had promised to take care of her, had told her it was okay to relax—believing him had turned into the worst mistake of her life.

She glanced down at her hands, twisted in the edge of the blanket Lil had brought her. The white scar along the base of the first three fingers on her right hand glared up at her, daring her to forget the first time Paul had showed up in a rage.

She'd waited for him for more than an hour under their tree in the center of the campus quad. She'd called his phone, but he didn't answer, so she'd gone back to her dorm room. When she'd arrived, he was standing next to her door, arms crossed over his chest and eyes ablaze.

"Where've you been?"

"I thought we were meeting in the quad."

"I was there, and you weren't."

"Of course I was. I was under our tree." She'd laughed as she unlocked the door and led him inside.

He hadn't said anything, and when she'd turned to him after throwing her purse on the double bed, his face had transformed. Once handsome, it had turned evil with his sneer.

"What's wrong?"

"I want to know who you've been with."

She'd put her hands on her hips and laughed in his face. "Right now? I was with the tree, waiting for you."

"Do you think this is funny?"

She'd giggled again, still not realizing just how angry he was. "A little bit. Why are you so mad?"

"You're out cheating on me with who knows who, and you're laughing about it?"

The tension in the tiny room had suddenly filled every corner. He was serious. Her voice turned soft but firm. "What are you talking about?"

"I won't let you mock me." His hand jerked back and came at her so fast that she'd only had time to raise her own hand in defense. Her right palm had taken the brunt of the keys he held in his own.

After, he'd knelt before her, holding a towel around her hand and begging her not to go to Student Health Services, where they'd ask a myriad of questions. She hadn't wanted to agree, but he'd been so sweet—so gentle and apologetic, swearing that he never meant to hurt her and that it would never happen again—that she had given in.

A sound near the doorway caught her attention. When she looked up, Matt's figure swam before her. Bending her neck, she rubbed her eyes quickly.

Matt settled next to her on the edge of the couch, his weight on the old cushion making her lean into him as he removed her melting ice pack and pressed a fresh one into place.

"How're you feeling?"

She blinked several times, afraid that her tears would give her away. She hadn't cried over Paul in years, and she had a feeling that this time had more to do with threatening notes and mounting stress than memories of that lowlife.

Matt tried again. "How's your head?"

"Better," she said. It wasn't exactly a lie—it *was* better than it had been before. But it still stung. Pain seared from temple to temple, concentrated over her left eye.

"Good." He brushed a loose strand of hair behind her ear. "There's something we need to talk about."

"Hmm?"

He stabbed his hand through his hair. "I've never said this to a girl before." Taking a deep breath, he continued on the exhale. "I think I should move in."

No headache in the world could have kept her from jerking her gaze up to meet his as she pulled back. The ice pack landed heavily in her lap, immediately leaking onto her blanket. "That's not funny, Matt," she said as she fumbled with the damp towel.

"I'm not kidding, Ashley." He used her name the same way she'd said his—making this whole conversation far too personal. But he didn't stop there as he put a hand on her knee. "There was a note on the brick."

"Another one? Why didn't you tell me?"

"I didn't want to worry anyone else in case they overheard."

That was probably a smart thing to do. Or not do. But it didn't make her any happier. "What did it say?" Matt swallowed, a battle waging on his face. "You can tell me the whole truth. Don't sugarcoat this for me."

"All right. He wants his property back, or he's going to take one of your girls."

Her ears began to ring, and her head felt too heavy for her neck to hold up any longer, so she let it fall against the couch cushion.

Matt scooped up her hands, swallowing them in his grip. "I'm not going to let anything happen to you or to anyone else here. I promise. I'll figure out who's behind this, and I won't rest until he's behind bars and can't bother you anymore."

His words were meant to comfort; instead they sent her back to that dorm room almost four years ago, to the promises Paul had made. Promises she'd *wanted* to believe, even when she knew in her heart of hearts that they weren't true. She'd been too weak to stand up for herself then.

She wasn't now.

He squeezed her hands with just enough pressure to remind her he still held them, drawing her attention to his gaze. Instead of a sneer, Matt offered brows furrowed in concern. Instead of cold eyes, he gazed at her with a warmth that filled her chest. Instead of clenched fists, his thumb moved in soothing circles on the back of her hand.

Matt wasn't Paul.

He wasn't out to control her or demand her submission.

That didn't mean she could just let him handle this. Not on his own. They'd manage together, or he'd go back to San Diego. She wouldn't sit back and let a man—even a good man—take over her life.

Never again.

She stared at him hard, praying that he could understand the message conveyed by every beat of her heart. "We. We'll find him. Together."

His wink was slow, filled with affirmation. "Then I can stay here?"

"We'll have to make sure everyone's okay with it, first. But if they don't mind, then…" She took a deep breath, bracing herself for what she was about to say, for the way she was about to make herself vulnerable. "Yes."

EIGHT

Ashley slapped at her beeping alarm clock, missing several times before it finally turned off, leaving her to the quiet of her tiny bedroom that was supposed to be peaceful. That *would* have been peaceful if it weren't for the rock the size of Coronado Island in her stomach.

She pressed her hand to her abdomen, trying to sooth the irritation, but it only served to move the knot that much closer to the front of her mind.

Maybe it had something to do with the way her home—the place she'd tried so hard to make safe for the women and children in her care—had been invaded the night before. It was just a brick that had entered the house, not the man who'd been threatening her himself. But the presence of his cruelty, his utter disregard for anything but his own agenda, drained the serenity from her haven. He'd intruded on their home and scared all of them. No amount of sweeping up glass shards or boarding up windows could change that. If she closed her eyes and held her breath, she could almost hear his footsteps as he watched over them. She suspected everyone else felt the same way. It was the only explanation for why they'd agreed to let Matt stay overnight.

Still, it hadn't been a comfortable discussion. Carmen's eyes had been like saucers when the idea was first offered, and she'd shaken her head like just the thought of a man under their roof put them all in danger. But Lil had encouraged the women to welcome Matt into the house from the start. She knew at least the basics of the threats and that Matt was trained to handle situations like this.

"There's been some vandalism in the neighborhood, and now it's hit home." The trill in her voice had risen as she pointed toward the front door. "In order for all of us to stay safe, we need to have an extra set of eyes here at all times."

"What about the police? Why can't they keep us safe?" Carmen's questions had echoed in the faces of the other two women.

Ashley had stepped forward then, still a little shaky on her feet, and clung to Lil's hand. "The chief has assured us that he's doing everything he can, but there are only a few officers." She'd run her fingers over the bandage covering the scratch on her forehead, the pinch of pain a reminder of the lengths to which her pursuer was willing to go. "He can't have an officer parked outside all night every night."

Up until that point in the house meeting, Matt had stood off to the side, hands grasped in front of him in a modified parade rest. So when he spoke, every head had snapped in his direction. "I've had the privilege of spending a few minutes with you and your families over the last couple days. I see how much you love each other and how much Ashley and Lil care about you. And I just want to help, if I can."

"Matt has received some training in self-defense," Ashley had explained, ignoring the way Matt's lips quirked at the massive understatement. "So he's ready to help if something should happen."

"Like what? What might happen?" It had been Benita's turn to voice her concerns as she'd hugged her son to her chest.

Ashley had swallowed down the words threatening to spill out. These women didn't need the whole truth. They were just learning how to live without daily fear. How could she convince them of the need to have Matt in the house without pushing them back several steps in the healing process?

Before she could respond, Greta had whispered, "Will he color with me again?"

"And play games with us?" Julio had joined in. "And maybe play catch with the baseball?"

Matt hadn't said anything, only nodded at each of the kids. Without even realizing it, he'd laid the groundwork for his acceptance into the house just by being himself. He'd earned the trust of the kids, who'd looked up at their mothers with pleading eyes. The moms hadn't had a chance.

She was glad that Matt was there. But even his presence wasn't enough to convince her she was safe. Not after a night spent alternately tossing and turning in bed and running scared through terrifying dreams. Maybe a hot shower would help.

She slipped on her robe over her pajamas and gathered her things, tiptoeing down the dark hallway past several closed doors. Just before slipping into the bathroom, she ventured a glance down the far hall toward the laundry room where they'd set up a cot. The door stood open wide; Matt's frame filled the entire space.

From the distance, she couldn't make out his expression or read his eyes. With arms crossed and back straight, he looked like a sentry keeping guard. Which was exactly what he was. Suddenly the rock in her stomach felt just the slightest bit smaller.

Heat blossomed in her cheeks, and she nodded at him

quickly before ducking into the bathroom and closing the door behind her.

When she emerged twenty minutes later, the rock in her stomach had dwindled even further, if not completely vanished. Clean and ready to face the day, she glanced toward the laundry room again. The door still stood open, but Matt had disappeared. She scooted toward the opposite wall to get a better angle into the room, but she could only make out the edge of the cot. No sign of Matt.

As she folded her pajamas and slipped them under her pillow, the phone in her office rang. Ducking across the hall, she picked up the receiver. Who could be calling so early in the morning?

"Lil's Place. This is Ashley."

"Ashley Sawyer?" The voice on the other end of the line was tight, as though the woman speaking was barely moving her lips.

"Yes. Can I help you?"

"This is Diane Smotherton. I'm a friend of Miranda's."

Her stomach pitched. They didn't have room for another family right now, but maybe they could shuffle a few beds and make room for a single woman.

"Miranda said she spoke with you yesterday, and…" The woman's voice trailed off. "Did she say anything?"

Ashley's thoughts derailed as she realized this wasn't a typical phone call. Usually when a woman said she was a friend of Miranda's, it was an opening to the part where she admitted that she needed a safe place to stay. This was shaping into something completely different, but why?

Ashley rubbed her hands down her jeans, giving herself a moment before responding. "About what?"

"I'm not sure. But it's just not like her to not show up." Diane's voice rose until she took an audible breath.

"Not show up where?"

"She was supposed to babysit for me so I could make my shift at the grocery store."

The dwindling rock in her midsection tripled in size, pushing the air out of her lungs, so that her response was more breath than actual words. "When did you last talk with her?"

"Last night. We set it up that she would be at my house at seven this morning to watch my son. But she hasn't showed."

The note. The note on the brick said that one of her girls would be taken. She'd been so sure that that meant one of the girls staying at the house. But Miranda was a volunteer, a friend—someone who supported Lil's Place and the work done there in a dozen different ways. She was one of Ashley's just as surely as if she lived under her roof. And now she might be paying the price for it.

Breathing in through her nose and letting it slip past her lips, Ashley chided herself. She was jumping to conclusions. Maybe Miranda had just overslept. "Did you call her?"

"Three times at home and twice on her cell phone. No answer, and her cell just goes straight to voice mail."

"Have you called the police?"

Diane squeaked, "Do you think that's necessary?"

She couldn't call the police until she was absolutely sure something was wrong. There was no leniency in her position for crying wolf. "I'm sure she just forgot and is in the shower or something." She nearly choked on the words that felt so much like a lie even as she desperately tried to convince herself that they were true. "I'll run by her place this morning and check on her."

"Thank you. Would you have her call me when you talk with her?"

"Sure thing. What number should I have her call?"

After scribbling the number on a sticky note, hanging up the phone and snatching her purse from its chair, she headed toward Lil's room—and ran smack into a wall of muscle in the entryway instead.

"Ash, what's going on? You're shaking." Matt's hands held tightly to her shoulders, his thumbs massaging her arms in slow circles.

"It's about Miranda. She's…I don't know where she is. She's not where she said she'd be. I think there's something wrong." She pointed at her office, trying to find the words to explain the situation as her mind filled in every possible evil scenario. "I have to go. I have to check on her."

"We'll go together."

She pushed against the soft cotton T-shirt covering his chest, trying to find more room to breathe, the band around her lungs pulling tight. "What about—" she took a quick breath "—the others here?"

"We'll let Lil know where we're going, and we'll ask them to stay in."

"But it's Sunday. They'll expect to go to church."

"We'll have a little service when we get back."

She blinked twice. Why wouldn't he just let her go?

A little voice reminded her they were in this together. She wasn't going to let him run off alone, and apparently he wasn't going to let her either.

"All right."

Despite the ringing in her ears, she managed to hear most of Matt's conversation with Lil. He used bland words like "checking in on" and "give her a hand" and never once let on the real reason for their impromptu trip. "Since Ashley and I won't be able to join you and the others for church this morning, maybe it would be best to skip services. We can have a little Bible study here in the living room this afternoon."

His phrasing was so innocuous, but the intensity of his gaze spoke volumes.

Lil nodded quickly, her loose, white curls bobbing around her ears. "I understand. We'll wait for you here."

Matt squeezed a wrinkled hand, and Ashley immediately felt a loss, as though he should be comforting her instead. "Thank you, Lil. We'll be back as soon as we can."

He wrapped an arm around Ashley's shoulder, ushering her toward the door and locking it behind them before racing her down the front walk.

Silence hung like a wool blanket over them as they sailed toward Miranda's house.

Matt swept his gaze over Ashley one more time. She sat perfectly still, as though afraid that if she even breathed, she'd fly apart. One of her arms was wrapped around her stomach; the other hung at her side. Her hand lay palm up on the gray-and-green plaid seat, lost and lonely.

Without letting himself think about any of the implications of his actions, he set his hand on top of hers. Her fingers wiggled their way between his until she held on to him with a sure grip, never once looking at him.

Still more than fifteen minutes from Miranda's place, he had to break the silence or they'd both go crazy playing what-if scenarios in their minds.

"So you never told me. How'd you end up at Lil's?"

She shot him a look that seemed to ask if this was really the best time to be talking about it, but when he nodded, she acquiesced. "My degree at UC Davis was in social work, and I just always knew that I wanted to help kids find safe homes."

"Why not work for the state?" They needed more good social workers who really cared about the kids in the system. At least they had when he was a kid. Almost certainly they still did.

"That's what I planned on at first."

Even after a hand squeeze, she didn't continue. "So what changed your mind?"

This time she peeked at him out of the corner of her eye, something like shame flashing across her face. "I guess I just realized that there were others in need." She looked away again, speaking toward the closed window. "You know that verse in the Bible about how serving the most down-and-out people is a way to serve God?"

"Sure." It was a favorite verse of his pastor.

"I couldn't stop thinking about that when I heard about Lil's. If ever there were women and children in need, it's these families. And even though there's never enough money, and there are never enough volunteers, at least I know that I've given everything I can to these women who need my help the most. For the two or three or more weeks they're with me, I don't regret serving them."

Strange. He'd thought the same thing about his own job. Caring for the poor. Defending the helpless. Fighting for the weak.

His job just usually required an international trip and involved fast roping from a helicopter.

"How'd you even hear about Lil's?" He stopped at a light and really looked at her as she watched something outside the window, her toe tapping against the floorboard.

"A friend of mine told me about it, said Lil might need some help."

"So you picked up everything and moved?"

She lifted a shoulder and frowned. "Pretty much."

There was more to her story than she was telling him, but this wasn't the time to pick at her for details. It was clear that his attempt to distract her hadn't worked at all.

The light turned green, and he floored it down the two-lane road, still several minutes from Miranda's house.

His palm turned damp, but only the one holding Ashley's hand. It took more than this to make him sweat, so he was pretty sure the moisture wasn't coming from him. He squeezed her fingers. "Are you worried about this? Because it's going to be all right."

"I know." She sounded like she was trying to convince herself—and doing a lousy job of it.

"Hey, Ash. Look at me." He took his eyes off the road long enough to meet her pained gaze. "I'm not going anywhere. I'll be here to see this through until this guy is caught."

She nodded, squaring her shoulders and putting on a brave face. It was the right response, just not the one he really wanted.

Why couldn't she stop putting on a show and just be real with him?

She was brave and strong all the time. More grit than grace. Never letting herself break down. Matt had seen a few guys like that in the service. If they needed to fall apart but never let themselves break in even the smallest ways, then when the walls finally came down they couldn't stop crumbling.

There wasn't time to dig into this either as he cranked the wheel into Miranda's driveway and parked next to her sedan. He wasn't sure if it was a good sign or not that her car was still there. The sour-sweet tension of pending action built in his stomach.

He caught up to Ashley on the steps to the front door. Which stood wide open.

He clamped a hand on her shoulder. "Stay behind me."

Her eyes shot toward the door then back to him, the corner of her lower lip clasped between her teeth as she nodded. Her hand fisted into his sweater just as it had at the bar.

As he nudged the door with his elbow, it swung into the living room.

Papers littered the hardwood floor. Sofa cushions had been pulled from their spots and flipped over. A lamp in the far corner had fallen from its stand, leaving the pieces of a shattered lightbulb in its wake.

"Miranda? Are you here?" Matt's voice filled the whole first floor, echoing from room to room as they waited for a response.

"That's her car out front," Ashley whispered. "And she lives too far off the beaten path to have walked anywhere. Where is she?"

"I don't know." He stepped into the living room, opening the door of the coat closet and chastising himself for not having a weapon. What had he been thinking leaving the house without his SIG?

Walking through an unknown house, completely unarmed, wasn't the big problem. Few promptly treated bullet wounds would actually kill a man. He should know. He'd had three of them.

Taking down an armed assailant wasn't really a problem either.

The serious issue with this situation was walking right behind him. Taking down a gunman without exposing her to danger? That was tricky. Feasible—just a little more difficult.

Keeping his mind on the closed doors yet to be opened and not on the fragile knuckles that kept grazing the small of his back?

Well...*that* was pretty near impossible.

They slipped into the kitchen on the far side of the living room, and he opened every pantry and cupboard door.

Back through the living room and up the stairwell, his eyes never stopped sweeping the area.

When they reached the top landing, a cry came from the bedroom straight ahead, and he yanked on Ashley's hand until she was clean against his back. Peering over his shoulder, he pressed his finger to his lips, and she nodded her cheek into his shirt. The cry had sounded more like a pet than a person, but he wasn't taking any chances—not with Ashley's safety at stake.

Blood rushed through his veins, propelling him toward the closed door, but he held back, taking another deep breath and wrapping an arm around Ashley. They moved in silence until the door handle clicked.

Another cry pierced the air, and he yanked the door open.

Just in time for a fat, orange tabby cat to bolt past them.

The rest of the room, including the closet, was empty. As was the rest of the upstairs.

"I don't know if I should be worried that she's not here or thankful that we didn't find her body." Ashley had let go of his shirt and put at least three steps between them as they walked back down to the living room. Her words were soft, and somehow they defied the pain in her voice.

"There's no sign that she was injured here, so let's pray that she was just taken to scare you. At least she doesn't know where Joy is."

"I know."

He pulled his cell out of his pocket, thankful he'd programmed the police station number into it. "I'm calling the chief to report her missing."

"Charity Way P.D." The gruff voice on the other end sounded like it needed another cup of coffee.

"I'd like to speak with Chief Donal."

"He's not here."

Matt turned to keep his eye on Ashley as she wandered through the ransacked room. "This is an emergency. Can you tell me how I can reach him?"

"Do you need me to send an ambulance?"

"No. Nothing like that. But a woman's been taken."

The desk sergeant rustled several papers. "How long's she been missing?"

"Since this morning at least. Maybe last night."

"I can take her name and get her in the system. And we'll have the next available officer look into it."

"How soon might that be?"

The sergeant sounded bored. "Maybe twenty-four or forty-eight hours."

Seriously? Ashley could be attacked again and Miranda could be dead in two days. They didn't have that kind of time to waste.

He stabbed his fingers through his hair, wishing his leg was up for a boxing session or a five-mile run. Any kind of physical activity really. Just something to take his mind off this twisted mission.

"Thanks." He hung up the phone just as the sergeant was asking for his name. "Looks like it's just you and me. But I have the chief's cell number back at the house with the rest of my stuff. Let's go back and make sure everyone's okay."

Back in his truck, they sped along toward Lil's, the rumble of the old engine and occasional creak of the seat springs the only sounds in the cab.

She was probably thinking about what had happened to Miranda. And she should be. But that wasn't nearly as important as figuring out what Joy knew. Because now there were three women in imminent danger.

They were still on the country road. Matt glanced into his rearview mirror as an inky-blue Suburban picked up speed, narrowing the gap between their two cars. His entire body clenched with instinct.

"Hang on to something," he said as he pressed on the old accelerator. The truck roared at his demand, but it wasn't going to be enough to outrun the sleek V8 engine behind them.

Ashley twisted around, staring into the SUV's grille as it bore down on them. "Who is that?"

Her words were high and her question empty. She already knew who was behind the wheel of the other vehicle as she swung forward and clung to the door handle with white knuckles. She had to know it was the same guy who had sent a brick through her window and cracked her windshield.

He'd been satisfied with distant threats before, but apparently not anymore.

"This could get bumpy." He let out a slow breath and swerved, the Suburban mirroring his movements as it eliminated the space between them. Its giant engine revved, and he only had time to yell, "Hold on!" as he flung his arm in front of Ashley before it crashed into the truck's rear bumper.

NINE

Ashley threw her hands up to the dashboard to stop herself from flying forward, but it was Matt's arm, which slammed into her chest, that held her in place as the truck lurched. Metal shrieked against metal as her head whipped forward.

She managed to turn her neck far enough to catch sight of the giant SUV as it pulled back. Matt shifted into a lower gear to give the pickup more power, then crushed the gas pedal.

"What are they doing?" Her voice squeaked, and she cleared her throat.

"Trying to get us to pull over."

His voice was as calm as if he were having a lazy Sunday afternoon on the beach. Didn't he know they were in trouble? That Suburban wasn't politely asking them to pull over. The driver wanted something. Actually, the driver wanted some*one*.

Her.

She swallowed the rising bile in her throat and took two big gulps of air. "What are we going to do?"

"Stay on the road."

Again with the clipped responses. Again with the freakish calm. His knuckles weren't even white as he steered the truck into the lane for oncoming traffic. Granted there weren't any cars coming at them, but she still grappled for the handle on her door. Anything to hold on to.

His right knee bounced to a tune she couldn't hear over the ringing in her ears. Her heart pounded, its speed rivaling the trees rushing by along the side of the road.

The Suburban pulled alongside them, and she stared into the tinted black window, searching for a face or anything else recognizable.

Suddenly the SUV veered into their lane.

Matt swerved at the same time, two wheels falling into the shoulder and sending gravel flying.

She could do nothing but try to catch her breath and hold on to her door for all she was worth. An attempt at asking God to keep them from a crash died on her lips as the truck started to slow.

She spun on Matt. "What are you doing? They're going to get in front of us."

"It's okay. I've got it under control."

The Suburban followed Matt's lead, slowing down just enough to keep the vehicles parallel, still racing down the two-lane country road.

"Are you ready?"

Before she asked what she needed to be ready for, he jammed his foot against the accelerator, and they sailed in front of the SUV.

"Hang on to something," he said as he cranked the wheel back toward the right lane. The Suburban clipped the passenger's side of the back bumper, spinning the truck until it faced the opposite direction.

She closed her eyes as they spun, willing her stomach not to fall victim to the instant nausea, her hands still grasping the door handle so tightly that they were starting to go numb.

Tires somewhere squealed, but they weren't the ones on the truck. As if he'd done the same thing every day of his life, Matt spun the wheel until they were in the right lane, flying back toward Miranda's house.

He was going at least twice the posted speed limit, his eyes jumping between the rearview mirror and the road in front of them. He had this under control, and all she had to do was not distract him or make it worse.

Just breathe.

Focus on the trees soaring by.

Keep her heart from flying out of her chest.

They passed Miranda's driveway without even a tap on the brakes, going miles and miles, turning onto obscure side roads until Matt swerved onto a cross street. He pulled mostly off the pavement and parked in the middle of the shallow ditch.

With both hands on the top of the wheel, he hung his head and let out two quick breaths. "Are you all right?"

Her clavicle was tender to her touch, and her seat belt had rubbed a spot on her neck raw. "Just fi-ine." She clamped her eyes shut as her voice broke, swallowing the urge to give into what had caused it, if just for a moment.

He didn't say anything else. Before she could look in his direction, his door slammed. "Matt?"

Her door squeaked as he wrenched it open and reached across her, undid her seat belt and lifted her to the ground without a word. His eyes had turned almost white, like ice; his hands were almost as cold as they ran over her arms, across her shoulders and up her neck. With deft movements, he inspected the back of her head, lifting her hair and then letting it slip back into place through his fingers. The chill that swept her skin had nothing to do with the fresh wind that kicked up the corner of her jacket.

"How's your neck feel? We should watch for whiplash."

"I'm all right. Really." She looked into his face and made the eye contact he'd been avoiding. "Are you?"

"Of course." He smirked as he backed up a step and dropped his hands to his sides.

She missed the contact immediately, mirroring him another two steps into ankle-deep grass. He watched her movements with narrowed eyes, lines deep between his eyebrows.

So this was Matt's version of panic. He'd been completely, eerily calm for the whole car chase, but now he was visibly shaken. That was very telling—it meant that it wasn't the dangerous situation that rattled him, but the possibility of harm coming to *her*.

And now that she'd put the pieces together, she wanted nothing more than to slide back into his arms—to comfort him while taking some comfort for herself as well. As if he knew what she was thinking, his nostrils flared twice followed by a very slow blink. A shake of his head seemed to tell her that they shouldn't. Couldn't.

Whatever he thought they shouldn't do didn't matter in that moment. She hadn't wanted anyone to hold her in years, hadn't wanted to be touched by any man in just as long. But in that minute she needed Matt to wrap his arms around her and hold on to her until her pulse returned to something resembling normal.

"We should get back to the house." His face wrinkled like it wasn't even close to what he wanted to do.

"I just need a minute."

Or an hour.

But how could she ask him to hug her fears away without admitting to them?

She bit into her bottom lip and raised her eyebrows. Maybe he'd understand. Maybe he'd be willing to admit that he needed a bit of contact to keep the ground from spinning away, too.

His cheeks puffed out as he let loose a slow breath, closing his eyes again and holding his arms out just enough to tell her it was okay.

No one had to ask her twice.

She stepped into his embrace, burying her face into his chest and breathing in the scents of his clean laundry and subtle aftershave. Hugging his waist with both arms, she wiggled a little bit closer as she laid her ear to his chest. The steady beats of his heart picked up speed until they matched her own, which still thudded as fast as they'd been driving.

"Your heart is racing."

His swallow reverberated all the way through her. "I know."

Her stomach churned with full-grown and not unwelcome butterflies. Lips tingling in anticipation, she waited. Hoping.

She wanted to kiss this man.

The realization plunged through her middle, leaving her almost breathless. She licked her lips with the tip of her tongue and prayed for a jolt of courage before looking up.

The infernal coolness in his eyes had thawed, replaced by something she'd never seen there before. Something that flicked and flickered like a flame.

In that moment Matt's jaw jerked, the pulse in his neck thumped and he dipped his head, leaving just a breath between their lips.

His aftershave was spicier this close to him. Maybe he tasted spicy, too.

She licked her lips again and pushed to her tiptoes until their lips met.

He dropped one of his arms from her shoulder to her

waist and moved the other so that he cupped the back of her neck, his fingers plunging into her hair.

Without a thought she lifted her hand to his cheek, his morning stubble in stark contrast with his curls at her fingertips. He leaned into her touch, scratching her chin with his whiskers but never letting go.

With shaking fingers, she grabbed the soft cotton of his shirt for support. And when her breath was completely gone, she pulled back and buried her face in the middle of his chest, avoiding any chance at eye contact.

What had she just done?

That was so stupid.

But the zing still on her lips and prickles down her spine didn't feel stupid. They felt like a warm robe on a cool morning. Like a cozy blanket in front of a roaring fire. Like she'd once dreamed it would.

Actually it was better than her sixteen-year-old dream.

This was real.

The man that she'd had a crush on then held her now and provided all of his protection.

He slowly pulled his fingers from her hair and ran his hand from the top of her head down to the back of her neck in smooth motions. His arm around her waist loosened, but he didn't let go. Did he know that if he did, she'd fall into a heap at his feet?

After several long minutes, her veins no longer felt like they were going to burst.

Matt's breathing had returned to normal, too, and he leaned away from her just far enough to look into her face. He hooked a finger under her chin and tilted it up. She couldn't make her eyes focus past his mouth as he cleared his throat and asked, "Okay?"

She bit her lip as she nodded.

"Ready to go back to the house now?"

Again, she could offer nothing but a mute nod.

Tristan was going to kill him.

Matt didn't have a chance in the world after kissing Ashley like that.

But, boy, had it been worth it.

He could still feel the way her lips had brushed his, hesitantly at first. But when her hands clutched at his shirt, she was all in, inhibitions and worries aside.

For a moment there on the side of the road, he'd forgotten about the Suburban and the man threatening Ashley. He'd lost all track of their surroundings and given up forming a single coherent thought.

He'd forgotten everything, including his own SEAL team number.

She fit in his arms like she'd been custom molded to be there. Holding her was like the answer to a prayer he'd never even prayed.

He'd survived a childhood that could have ruined him in so many ways. He'd gotten through Hell Week and been wet and sandy on the Coronado beach for eight weeks straight during SEAL indoctrination. He'd faced missions that had brought strong men to their knees.

But he'd go through it all again for another kiss like that.

Of course, if Tristan ever found out about it, he wouldn't live long enough to re-up with the teams. Tristan would have good reason, too.

He wasn't good enough for Ashley. He couldn't offer her much on his salary or give her nearly what she deserved. She should have beach-house vacations, diamond jewelry and a family. Even if he could ever afford the first two, the third was a bad idea for him.

He'd read the literature. He knew the statistics. Children raised in abusive homes were more likely to become abusers of their spouses and their own children. He'd had three foster dads who had chosen beatings as their preferred form of discipline.

Add to that long and often sudden overseas assignments. If he wasn't present—and making a mess of things—he'd be thousands of miles away, leaving his wife to wait in anxious silence for interminable days and weeks.

Any way he added it up, he'd make a rotten husband and father. Ashley and her someday children deserved much better than that.

But he could still enjoy the memory of holding her in his arms.

"Where are you going?" Ashley pointed down the cross street he should have taken to return to Lil's Place.

He'd missed his turn. Because he was daydreaming about kissing the girl sitting next to him again. "Just thought we should check the neighborhood for the Suburban before we go in."

If the wrinkle across her forehead was any indication, she didn't entirely buy that. Too bad—it had been a very good excuse, even if he'd had to come up with it on the fly.

There was no sign of the SUV on any of the surrounding streets or as he pulled up in front of Lil's, so they hopped out of the truck, hurrying toward the door.

Lil met them inside. "Were you able to help Miranda?"

Ashley shook her head, blond hair bouncing once at her chin. "She wasn't there."

Lil's face turned pale beneath her artificially rosy cheeks, and she lifted shaking hands to cover her mouth. "Gone?"

He didn't like the direction of this conversation. It wasn't going to do them any good to breed fear in such a small house, so he plastered a smile in place. "We'll take care of it. We'll find her." Lil seemed placated. But while Ashley's eyes said she desperately wanted to believe him, he knew she wouldn't be as easy to convince. She'd seen the house.

He nodded toward the living room. "Did someone say something about house church? Should we sing a few songs and read a few verses?"

Lil's white curls bounced in eager agreement as she scurried to collect the others. He reached for Ashley's elbow, giving it a quick squeeze, then immediately jerked back. Touching in any capacity was a bad idea.

"I'll go call the chief and tell him about the Suburban. Unless you'd rather go to the station to file a report?"

"No. I don't want to go anywhere right now, except to the couch."

He excused himself to go place the call from his make-shift bedroom, but when he punched in the chief's cell phone number, it went straight to voice mail.

"This is Chief Donal. Leave a message, and I'll get back to you."

How to light a fire under the cop without scaring the daylights out of him? "Donal, this is Senior Chief Waterstone. I think we have a situation involving Miranda Cain. Also, Ashley and I ran into a little trouble on Highway 492 today not far from Miranda's place. Call me back."

"You're squeezing me too tight."

Ashley jumped at the words whispered in her ear, immediately loosening her arms around the little girl sitting in her lap. "Sorry," she whispered back.

Greta smiled and snuggled back into place, her blue eyes trained on Matt's face on the opposite side of the circle.

He sat on a kitchen chair, reading from the open Bible in his hands and looking like he had home church every week.

Then again, maybe he did.

The SEAL schedule didn't usually allow for weekends off, so his study of God's Word was probably less formal than her normal Sunday schedule.

He glanced up in the middle of a sentence and caught her eye, sending her heart into overdrive and her mind right back to the side of the road just a few hours before. Was he thinking about the same thing?

He ruffled his hair in the sudden silence, every eye in the room on him. He cleared his throat and looked back down into his hands. "Sorry. Where was I?" His finger scanned the page. "Right. Verse nine. 'But He said to me, 'My grace is sufficient for you, for My power is made perfect in weakness.' Therefore I will boast all the more gladly about my weaknesses, so that Christ's power may rest on me.'"

He kept reading, but her ears filled with the roar of the words he'd just spoken, repeated over and over again.

My power is made perfect in weakness.

But not now. Not in this situation. This wasn't a time for weakness. With Miranda missing and Joy and all of her girls and guys in danger, this was no time to sit back. She had to be strong for them. They deserved her very best to protect them.

Matt closed his Bible. She hadn't heard anything he'd read, except that one verse, which didn't really apply for the time being.

He pulled out her tattered hymnal from beneath his chair. "Let's see. What's one that we all know?"

"'A Mighty Fortress'!" Julio bounced on the couch next to her.

Matt agreed with a smile, his clear baritone soon filling the room as he led them in three verses of the old song. She stumbled on the words, but kept her eyes on Greta so she wasn't more distracted than she had to be.

She couldn't afford another distraction. Matt was supposed to be helping her, not making it harder for her to find the man responsible for threatening her home and the people in it.

She just wouldn't think about him any more than she had to. That would be easy enough. She hadn't really thought about a man in years. Until Matt showed up.

How hard could it be to go back to that state of mind? How hard could it be not to dwell on the way his arms fit just right around her waist? She just had to go back to that time right after Paul, when the pain—both physical and emotional—had been so fresh that she'd removed herself from the world just to survive.

She'd done what she had to, and she'd do it now, too. It was for the best, right?

Matt marched the nine feet from wall to wall of the laundry room, his socks barely making a sound on the powder-pink, linoleum floor.

A few verses of "A Mighty Fortress Is Our God" out of Ashley's ancient hymnal; chapter twelve from Second Corinthians in the New Testament; and a rousing game of Crazy Eights with Greta, Julio and company that afternoon hadn't done much to soothe his nerves. And now that everyone else had gone to bed, the hair on the back of his neck wouldn't lie back down.

He stopped moving and sniffed the air. Something more than the line-dried scent of fabric softener floated into the room. Cracking open the door, he peered through the opening, but the night-light in the bathroom at the opposite end of the hall couldn't penetrate the shadows.

As he pushed the door just far enough to slip past, it let out a screech of anguish, and he stilled, not even taking a breath in the stillness.

Just when it was safe to move again, a light illuminated the kitchen. With completely silent motions, he walked toward it, ducking his head around the corner of the door frame.

Julio tilted a carton of orange juice away from his mouth, his guilty gaze making it over the bottom edge of the container. "I was thirsty." The little boy's voice shook, and he flinched away as Matt stepped into the doorway.

It was like looking in a twenty-year-old mirror. The same protective movements, jerky motions and fearful eyes.

He fought the sudden desire to scoop the kid up and hug the fear out of him. *Dear Lord, why does anyone have to live through this? I just don't get it sometimes.*

Clearing his throat, he asked, "Did you see someone else do that?"

"My dad." The whispered words punched Matt in the gut. "He used to drink milk like this, too."

"Did he ever catch you drinking out of the carton?"

Julio blinked several times, his chin wobbling up and down. "He told me it was something only men did. But Mom told me I had to be the man of the house now."

Matt fell to his knees in front of the boy and squeezed him in a bear hug, the almost empty juice carton crumpling between them, and ruffled the dark brown hair that hung over the collar of the boy's fire-truck pajamas. "Tell you what. This'll be our secret." He took the juice and tipped it back, draining the last of it. "But next time, we'll both get cups."

"'Kay."

He leaned back, once again running his hand over the baby-soft hair. "Now get back to bed." Julio scampered back to his bedroom, his feet slipping on the pajama pants that were at least three inches too long.

He'd never spent much time with children in the past. There had been a few foster siblings here and there, but Tristan and Ashley and their mom were his only real family. So why had the run-in with Julio felt that natural? It just made sense to comfort the kid, to hug him until his fear vanished. It was easy to see the boy wasn't hurting himself or anyone else, so there wasn't a need to tell anyone else.

The phone in his pocket vibrated, and he hurried into the laundry room before answering the call from the unavailable number. "Waterstone."

"Matty."

"Tristan. What's going on?"

"You know how it is. Just waiting for a ride to the insertion point. Only have a few minutes." His voice sounded more like it had traveled from the moon than the eight thousand miles actually between them. That was just part of communicating from a Middle Eastern op. "How's Ash?"

"Fine. Good. She's great." He scrubbed a hand down his face. Could he possibly sound like more of an idiot? Tristan was going to know something was up.

"So you found the guy who sent her that note."

Right. The note. The reason he was in Charity Way. "Not yet."

In the ultimate lieutenant tenor, Tristan said, "How serious is it?"

"Listen, she's going to be fine. This guy's not that smart, and I'm not going to leave her side." Sure, he wasn't leaving her side, but there was more to it than a crazy guy writing letters and threatening innocent women.

He just didn't know what it was.

"You're sure?"

"Absolutely. I've got this under control." *Mostly,* he amended silently.

Tristan covered the mouthpiece as someone shouted behind him in Arabic. He responded in kind, as though he'd been speaking the language his whole life. That's why he was the team's linguistics specialist.

"We're going wheels up in ten, so I've got to go, but will you watch out for her?"

"I will. I *am.*"

"I know. I know. And hey, keep your eyes out for bad-news boyfriends, too."

"Oh, really?" His own words tried to strangle him as Ashley's face flashed on the backs of his eyelids. Would Tristan hear the guilt in his voice? Could he know that this side of 8:00 a.m. Matt had been kissing Ashley as if he never planned to quit?

"You know how it was with that college jerk."

Matt sat down hard on his cot, the aluminum legs squeaking angrily. "What jerk?"

"Come on, you remember. The one who thought he could give her a black eye and a broken rib and get away with it."

He lost the ability to breathe and managed only a negative grunt.

"What was his name?" Tristan snapped his fingers three times. "Peter. Pedro. Paul. Something like that."

Matt sucked in several quick breaths, trying to make sense out of any part of the story. "What happened to him?"

"Well, you were there."

"I don't think so." He'd definitely remember teaching a jerk like that the lesson of a lifetime.

"Hmm. Maybe it was Zach. Anyway, we just gave him a little practical demonstration of what it was like to be a punching bag for someone bigger and stronger than him."

Ashley had been abused by her college boyfriend. That's why she hadn't gone into the state system as a social worker. It's why she watched over the women of Lil's with such intensity. She knew their pain firsthand.

What a woman.

It took someone incredibly special to take her pain and turn it into service to others. But that's what she'd done. It was amazing what she'd done here in Lil's Place, how she'd overcome her own fear and anguish to make a safe place for the people who needed it.

A safe place where he didn't belong at all.

"I've got to run. But watch out for my little sister, okay? She doesn't need any more broken bones or another broken heart."

TEN

Matt opened his eyes at the first hint of the morning sun through the mini blinds meant to cover the window. He'd slept very little, rising at every noise and prowling through the house every hour. Burning eyes and aching shoulders weren't enough to keep him in bed, and he rolled up immediately, making his rounds.

The house slept, each groan of the floorboards and creak of a settling wall a gentle snore. The old house was worn out.

So was Ashley.

They had to wrap this up. Fast.

It would be better for Ashley in every respect if he could just find the guy making these threats and get back to San Diego. Then he wouldn't be tempted to imagine a life where kissing her every day wasn't a problem. A time when he could actually convince himself that they could have a relationship with neither of their pasts getting in the way.

Far-fetched as they were, he pictured those scenes and more as he walked into the kitchen and pulled out a carton of eggs. His specialty—actually the only meal at which he was competent—was southwestern scrambled eggs, so he cracked them open, pouring them into a bowl and beating the eggs with more vehemence than was technically required.

A life with Ashley, where she made him laugh and he protected her, played across the back of his eyelids, and he whipped harder. Dreams like that didn't come true for little foster boys like him. He'd learned how to fight hard and fight back. He'd learned how to suffer but endure the worst. The things he'd learned made him a good SEAL, a fearless warrior.

He'd never learned how to care for a woman. As a kid, he'd only seen one man model how to treat a woman well and raise a family.

Ashley deserved someone who knew these things.

He dumped a generous measure of salsa into the eggs and whisked them some more.

It'd be better to spend the morning figuring out their next steps to uncovering the lunatic than battling thoughts of a life that wouldn't ever be. Greta's fairy-tale princesses were the only ones that got happily ever afters.

The eggs sizzled as they hit the frying pan, and he stirred them slowly, going over everything he knew thus far.

Joy was safe. She'd been stashed and protected in a place that no one but Ashley knew. And whoever was after her was willing to go pretty far to get her back. Something serious was driving the other man. Serious enough that he was clearly willing to go through a lot of trouble to get his way, and he wasn't acting alone. The notes only seemed to come from one man—they all said "me" and "I", not "we" or "us"—but at least two people were involved in the attacks, with one driving the getaway car. Matt wondered if either one was the real villain. Whoever was writing the notes seemed intent on hiding his identity—would he really risk getting caught in the act?

The guy probably wasn't wandering through the neighborhood in the middle of the night, or even driving a blue Suburban. Most likely he had some goons doing his bidding. If he wasn't alone, how big was his organization? Was it a crime family? A local group of thugs? Or just a family trying to get their kid back?

Regular families didn't send threatening notes.

And it all somehow involved Miranda. No way had she given them a clue and then randomly disappeared after they received that note. It was far too many coincidences. She was wrapped up in this mess, even if she didn't want to be, which meant he had to go back to the last clue she'd given them.

How was the Infinity tied to the whole thing?

He tossed a few slices of bread into the toaster and pressed the button. The coils glowed pink instantly, and he warmed his hands over the rising heat. It was chilly in the house in December.

But it hadn't been cold inside the Infinity.

"Good morning."

Matt jerked at the voice, instantly ready for anything. Wrapped in a heavy gray sweater that covered her to her knees, Ashley lifted a hand to cover a yawn. Her fuzzy, pig-shaped slippers padded her steps as she shuffled to the coffeemaker and dumped in the grounds.

"Morning. You sleep okay?"

She nodded around another yawn. "You?"

"Fine. Talked to your brother last night."

Her eyes lit up, and all droopiness vanished. "How is he?"

"Great. They're all great." Longing pinched in his stomach. He should have been there, too. It was time to get back on the job. Get Ashley's situation wrapped up and get back to the teams. His leg felt better and with a couple more weeks of physical therapy, he'd be right there with them.

Away from thoughts that were consuming far too much of his time and would soon feature pink pig slippers.

"You looked pretty deep in thought there."

"Yeah. I was just thinking, it's kind of cold in here."

"Oh, well, we had a drop in donations this year, so I'm trying to save a few dollars a month by turning down the thermostat. Do you need another blanket for your bed?"

"I slept outside in the middle of the desert one night during a training op. It got down into the thirties. I think I can handle sixty-seven in here."

"Oh." She poured her coffee without looking at him.

"But it got me thinking. Who heats an abandoned building in the winter?"

She wrapped both hands around her mug and held it to her lips, blowing gently into the steaming java. "I don't know. Why do—" Her eyes flew open, and her gaze locked on his. "The bar. It was warm, wasn't it?" She shook her head, and he could see the pieces falling into place. "It was a pretty mild day, and the sun was shining, but it was really warm in there."

"I don't think it's abandoned at all. And what did your buddy say?"

"My buddy?" She gazed into the black liquid in her cup, as though it would give her all of the answers she needed. "They'd brought in some big equipment and moved some earth out of there."

"I think we missed something when we were there."

Her head bobbed quickly, and she motioned with her hand, sloshing coffee over the lip of the mug. She wiped up her spill, but before she could say anything more, the phone in her office rang. "I'd better get that."

He followed her into the foyer. As she disappeared

through the open door, the sun glinting off a midnight-blue vehicle caught his attention. He let her go and unlocked the front door before slipping outside.

Just as he thought. The blue Suburban was back. As it sailed around the corner, he could clearly see that the plates had been covered. They were being staked out.

While he waited for the SUV to return, a police cruiser pulled past. He trotted down the steps, his leg not even twinging in protest. The officer behind the wheel didn't glance in his direction.

The chief may have done what he said he'd do, but it wasn't going to do a lick of good if the cop didn't at least look in the direction of the house.

Just as he lifted a hand to wave down the officer, Ashley called out to him from the front doorway. "Matt. Matt, come quick."

He ran back to her, bounded up the stairs and grabbed for one of her hands. "What's wrong?"

"On the phone. The man on the phone." She gasped for a breath before pressing her eyes closed and biting her lip.

"What did he say, Ash? Who was it?"

She swallowed, fighting to keep her features neutral. "I don't know who it was. But he said he'd trade Miranda for Joy. He said if he didn't get Joy back, we'd never hear from Miranda again."

For a second, Matt looked just as stunned and shaken as Ashley felt. Then his take-charge SEAL mask fell in place. "What did you say to him?" he asked.

A tear leaked from under her closed lids, and she knuckled it away, gasping in surprise as Matt cupped her cheek and pulled her to his chest. She was glad when he steered them back into the foyer and closed the door behind them.

She was even happier that he managed to do so without letting her go.

"It's okay, Ash. It's all right to cry."

No, it wasn't. Didn't he understand that? What would the children think if they saw her crying? What would their mothers think? She couldn't let them see her breaking down. "I'm not crying," she said into his sweatshirt, even though the loud sniffle that followed said otherwise. Thankfully, he didn't press the point, instead rubbing big circles into her back. "I didn't know what to say to him, so I didn't say anything. He said that he'd be in touch again and then he hung up."

"Okay. Not much to go on. Why don't we—" He paused, surprising her. Since when did he hesitate before telling her what he thought they should do? "What do you want to do?"

"I want to crawl back in bed and wake up four years ago before I'd ever even heard of Lil's."

Her ear rested on his chest, taking comfort in the steady thump of his heartbeat.

"Sorry, kiddo. My truck hasn't served as a time machine in a few years. We're going to have to keep moving forward."

Ashley looked up at him, then let her gaze drop back to the floor between her slippers as she chewed on her bottom lip. "I guess we better call the chief." After a shaky sigh, she said, "Then I want to know what's going on at the Infinity."

"Me, too." He patted her back several times. "I'm proud of you, Ash. You're doing a pretty amazing thing here."

She sure didn't feel amazing today. She was vulnerable and lost and shaken to the core. She shook her cheek against him. "No, I'm not. I'm just doing what has to be done." *And today, it doesn't feel like nearly enough.* Ash-

ley was usually pretty good at summoning confidence and
determination, but it felt like everything that had happened
over the past few days had whittled away her surety, leaving her the same fragile, unhappy girl who couldn't protect herself, much less anyone else.

"I'm serious," he said. "These women need you, and
after what you went through in college, to help them is—"

Every one of her muscles tensed, pulling her away from
his embrace, even though his arm still circled her shoulders. She jerked her head up, and looked anywhere but at
him. "What do you mean?"

"Um…just th-that—" He clearly realized he'd said the
wrong thing, but there was no backing away from it now.
Finally, the words she'd dreaded spilled out. "Tristan said
that there was a guy. Peter? He just… I mean, it takes a
lot of courage. You know you're very strong."

Her neck burned until her cheeks flamed and she
marched backward, putting a few feet between them. He
knew? Tristan had *told him?* She was so humiliated and hurt
she wanted to scream. She opened her mouth to say something, but the words weren't there, so she snapped it closed.

"I'm sorry." He was quick to apologize though she was
pretty sure he didn't know what he was apologizing for.
"I didn't know. I mean, I'm not quite sure. That is, your
brother just— Last night he said to—"

The more he said, the worse she felt. She had to get
away.

"I need to get cleaned up," she said and ran for the door.
If she hurried, she could be first in the shower. And with
the noise of the pounding water, no one in the house would
notice if she cried.

Showered, dressed and with her hair halfway dry, Ashley finally felt that she'd regained control of herself. Tears

weren't quite as close to the surface—now she was just mad. She waved her hair dryer like a weapon, wishing she could smack her brother with it. What had he been thinking spilling the whole story of Paul to Matt? She'd worked so hard to be strong since then, and then at her weakest moment, she got slammed by it all over again. Like she'd crawled up a staircase only to be pushed back down, reminded of all of her failings.

Her damp hair flopped in the burst of heat from the dryer—just like the rest of her life, going wherever the wind blew it. Or, more accurately, wherever the note writer sent it. But that was over, starting now.

She wasn't going to let someone steal everything she'd worked so hard for. Security. Peace of mind. Hope. These were hers, and she hadn't gotten them by lying down when things got tough. She was going back to that bar, and she was going to figure out what Miranda had been trying to tell her. Whatever Miranda had known had landed her in trouble, and there was no crying "uncle" while women were in danger.

Just as she turned off the dryer, someone thumped on her door twice. "Ashley? There are still some eggs on the stove," Matt called through the door. "I'm going to run into town and see if I can find out who owns the Infinity property. Maybe there'll be something to point us in the right direction."

Thankful that she'd dressed before drying her hair, she opened the door and stuck her head out. "I'll be ready to go in a second. Just let me grab my shoes."

"Maybe you should stay here." He had an expression that reminded her of when Julio broke something in the living room. He couldn't meet her gaze and instead hemmed and hawed with his hands behind his back and toe digging into the floor.

Just great. She'd made him uncomfortable. Or rather, her reaction to the bombshell he'd dropped on her, courtesy of her brother, had made him uncomfortable. Well, it wasn't going to keep her behind today.

"I'll be there in a minute." She slammed the door before he could argue and ran to find her tennis shoes.

Matt was waiting for her in the foyer, his arms crossed and forehead wrinkled, when she came out to join him. "Are you sure you want to go? It's probably going to be pretty boring."

"It's Monday. I can pick up my car today." She twirled her keys as she pulled her jacket from the hook by the front door. "Think you can handle a walk?"

She flung open the door and bounded down the steps without giving him a chance to respond, but he was by her side without missing a step.

They walked several blocks in silence, always keeping a respectable distance between them. His breathing, soft and consistent like a metronome, set the pace, and he matched his strides to hers.

As they turned the corner, a big orange house with an array of pink flamingos in the front yard loomed ahead. Matt looked at her with an arched brow. "Why don't you get some flamingos like that? I think they really add to the neighborhood."

"I'll look into that right away."

His smirk faded until his lips formed a thin line. "I'm sorry about this morning. I didn't mean to…um…bring up something you obviously didn't want to talk about."

"Thank you." And she meant it.

"I'm sorry, too, about what you went through."

So was she. That didn't mean she wanted to talk about it with him.

He jammed his hands into his pockets, clearly looking

for something to do. If she didn't steer this conversation, he was going to pick it up right where she didn't want him to.

"How's your leg feeling?"

If he'd been a porcupine, his quills would have fanned out. Apparently he wanted to talk about his leg almost as much as she wanted to talk about Paul. They needed a safer topic.

"Should we stop by the police station and talk with the chief?" She pointed toward their next turn.

"I called him this morning after breakfast." Matt didn't sound at all happy. "I told him about Miranda, and he was madder than we were. He said he'd look into it right away. And he asked me to keep my eye out and to call his cell if we see any sign of her."

"Did you say anything to him about the Suburban that tried to run us off the road?"

He shrugged. "I mentioned it, but without plates or any real evidence of a crime he can't do anything."

"What about the blue streak of paint on the tailgate of your truck?"

"What about the other four paint streaks? That truck's been hit more than a baseball. There's no way to prove the blue paint is from an illegal act without a witness or a serious accident."

How could he be so calm and rational about the whole thing? The blood beneath the surface of her skin simmered at the memory of the ordeal, but he acted as though it had been nothing. Like they hadn't narrowly escaped a serious accident.

Like he hadn't kissed the stuffing out of her right after they lost the SUV.

Oh, dear.

Why was she thinking about that again?

Maybe because he held you like that this morning but didn't make any move to kiss you.

She shoved open the door to the county recorder's office in an attempt to silence the snotty voice in her head. No need to be thinking things like that.

A slim woman in an ill-fitting, but not altogether unflattering navy suit stood behind the counter, her elbows on the counter and chin resting in her hands. The blue sign perched on the ledge said Sandy Brummings. "Help you?"

"Yes, please. Can you tell us who owns—"

A door at the end of the hall slammed open into the adjacent wall, and a man with a vaguely familiar face—and even more memorable sleek black hair—stumbled into the hallway, pulling on a brown overcoat as he yelled over his shoulder, "I'll be back after the game." The feminine voice inside the office said something else that she couldn't understand. "Hold my calls. It won't take more than a couple hours."

Matt leaned in to speak to the clerk as the other man ducked down a side hallway. "Who is that man?"

"That's the mayor," Ashley said.

Sandy nodded, then winked like they shared a secret. "Off for his weekly poker game with Chief Donal and a few local business owners, I suppose. His office and the county offices share a parking garage, so he comes through here like that regularly." They all looked back at the spot where the politician had vanished.

Ashley cleared her throat, bringing them back to the present. "So can you tell us who owns some property?"

"What land?"

"It's at the corner of Simpson and Elm. It used to be a bar called the Infinity."

Sandy's one-inch fingernails clacked against the keyboard of her computer, her face a composition of concentration. "You folks thinking about buying it?"

They'd been asked that before.

"Just checking it out." Matt offered the same response as he had to the tipsy man.

"Well, it looks like the property was purchased a little over a year ago."

Just like the old guy had said.

Sandy tapped one fingernail against her teeth, sucking on it as her eyes went back and forth across the screen. "It's owned by a company called Ithyka Inc."

"How do you spell that?" Ashley dug in her purse for a scrap of paper, but couldn't even find a pen before the other woman scribbled it onto a sticky note. The blue paper stuck between her nails, waving like a flag in a hurricane.

"Thank you."

Matt leaned an elbow on the counter, bending his considerable height until he drew even with Sandy. "Do you know anything about this Ithyka Inc.? Any idea who owns it?"

Sandy's eyelashes beat faster than hummingbird wings as she smiled into Matt's handsome face. She licked her red lips twice, flashing white teeth at him. "I could check on that for you."

He grinned, lines forming at the corners of his eyes in a true smile.

Ashley pressed her hand to her stomach over a sudden knot. When had it gotten so hot inside? She ran a finger around her collar trying to get some air.

"That's all right, Ms. Brummings. Thank you for your time."

She marched ahead of him into the street after a quick wave at the clerk. If it hadn't been for his footsteps, she wouldn't have been sure he was with her until they reached the cool air where she could breathe again.

"Are you okay?"

"Fine." She pushed a short breath through her nose. "But what were you—" She took a deep breath, trying to calm herself down—a task that became significantly more difficult when she looked at his face, where a slow grin formed.

He pointed at the closed door and raised both eyebrows. "Ashley, were you—"

Jealous.

The unspoken word hung in the air for hours. At least for long moments of painful silence.

Because it was so terribly, utterly true.

Finally she just turned and walked toward the glass repair shop. She had no words to explain her reaction to a completely innocent interaction. She had no right to be jealous of anyone where Matt was concerned. He'd be leaving town shortly. In no time at all this whole ordeal would be over, and she'd be back to life on her own.

Yet despite her rationalizations, she still couldn't come up with anything to say as they picked up her car and drove the nine blocks back to Lil's. He seemed to understand that, letting the quiet keep them company.

When she parked behind his truck, the blue stain on the tailgate taunted her, and she brushed her hand on it as she walked around the front of her car. This would end. It couldn't go on forever.

It had to end soon.

Matt leaped from the passenger seat when the telltale crack of a gunshot split the air, and the car window next to them exploded.

ELEVEN

Matt snatched for Ashley's hand, which was still raised to cover her ear, and yanked her to his side, low to the ground. They squatted over the glass that was strewn across the street, sheltered by the little coupe's door on one side and the passenger seat to his back.

He wrapped both of his arms around her as she tucked into his side. With eyes pinched closed she clutched at his arms, as though trying to pull a blanket tighter around her.

"That was a gunshot, wasn't it?" He had to read her lips, as her pitch was barely audible, especially to ears still ringing from the sudden gunfire.

She wasn't really asking a question. The sallow tint to her face told him she already knew the truth, but he answered her anyway. "Yes." He rubbed his hand in slow figure eights on her back, looking through the frame where the window had been for any sign of the shooter. Out of habit, he reached for the gun he always carried in his belt holster when on a mission. Except he wasn't on a mission. And there was no gun there.

He curled his fingers through the window opening and pulled himself up until he could take quick inventory of the situation. She trembled into his side as he eyed the spaces between every house and mentally checked off that every car had been there the previous three days.

Of course, the shot had missed her by ten inches. And if they were dealing with a pro, as Matt suspected, he wouldn't have missed. That meant that killing Ashley wasn't the shooter's goal. Whoever was after Joy knew the only way to get to her was through Ashley.

Someone wanted to send a message. It had worked.

He immediately ran quick hands from her shoulders to the tips of her fingers and from her knees down to the tops of her gray sneakers. "Are you bleeding? Were you cut?"

She shook her head, eyes still closed and lips quivering with every breath. But at least her shoulders rose and fell in a steady rhythm.

Letting out a slow breath seemed to loosen the knot in his stomach, and he reached for her cheek, desperately needing to feel her warmth and be assured she had been spared injury.

"I'm going to call the police, and we're going to wait here until they arrive and make sure it's safe to go out in the open. All right?"

Her shaking chin moved up and down against his shoulder, and he hugged her tighter as he pulled his phone from his pocket and dialed the station.

"Charity Way Police Department. This is Sergeant Andrews."

"Yes, this is Matt Waterstone. Someone shot at Ashley Sawyer outside Lil's Place."

"Is anyone injured?"

Only shaken up. "No. We're fine, but pinned down next to a black two-door."

"I'm sending officers there right now."

He hung up before the officer could ask him to stay on

the line. He didn't want to answer any more questions right now or think about anything except how to stop Ashley's lips from trembling.

Only every time he thought of how close he'd come to losing her, his limbs shook, too. So close to never seeing her smile again. He'd never be able to forgive himself if he didn't protect her.

This wasn't about a promise to Tristan anymore.

If he was honest, it hadn't been about that for a while now.

Finally she blinked at him, her eyes bluer than the Texas sky and warmer than a Middle Eastern summer. "Were you hit? Are you hurt?"

The pad of his thumb made a slow trail from her cheekbone to her jawline as she leaned into it. He tried to reassure her with a sad smile. "No. I'm fine."

She closed her eyes again, leaning her head on his shoulder, trusting him to care for her. No woman had ever trusted him like this. And it was more than just trusting him with her safety. By letting herself lean on him, she was trusting him with her vulnerability, too—trusting that he wouldn't take advantage of her moment of weakness. Trusting that he wouldn't hurt her.

Ashley kept trying to prove her strength. But maybe that wasn't what she needed. Hadn't that been in the Scriptures they read the day before? In human weakness God's strength can be shown. In this moment, he was glad to see that she wasn't forcing herself to stay strong.

She pressed her nose into his shoulder and sniffed a couple times. "Is he still out there?"

"Let's not risk it, just in case. The police will be here soon."

She smiled up at him, and his gut clenched in response.

This wasn't fear or anxiety but their cousin, yearning. Oh, he knew it well. He'd succumbed to it the morning before.

But not today.

No matter how much he wanted to kiss away her fear or soothe her nerves or hug the dread out of her.

He ran his hand over her hair in several long strokes, smoothing out a few wayward strands. But the partial smile she gave him had nothing to do with fixing her hair. His arms and hands shook, and he had a feeling it wasn't from the cold or the spike in adrenaline.

"Are you warm enough?"

She nodded, the tip of her tongue sweeping over her lips.

Just like the day before.

But that didn't mean he had to go there again.

She swallowed slowly and drew in a deep breath before whispering over his shoulder, "For a second, I thought I was going to lose you."

This was a bad idea.

Worse than before. So much worse.

Now there was no excuse. He knew what he was getting into, and there was no denying that Tristan would be furious.

"I'm so glad you're okay."

"Me, too," he replied. "Umm…I mean, I'm glad you're all right." What was it with this girl that made his tongue act like it had never spoken a clear sentence in his life? "We're both going to be fine."

"Why didn't you go after him?"

"I didn't see where the shot came from, and I wasn't going to wander the neighborhood without making sure you're protected."

"Thank you." Something flickered in her eyes, but she closed them too fast for him to identify it. She leaned toward him, seemingly about to press a kiss onto his cheek. Except she caught the corner of his mouth instead.

Danger. Pull back. Pull back.

The order rang in his head, but clearly he had his own issue with weakness, because when she started to lean back, there wasn't a thing he could do to stop himself from turning his head and pressing his lips to hers.

She melted into his arms, warm and comforting. Her kiss wiped away every fear that sprang to mind.

Maybe it could always be like this. Maybe this is what he'd been holding out for. Maybe he'd just been waiting for the right girl.

Sirens belted into the quiet street, and he jerked back to a perfect view of her bright red lips.

Or maybe he should get on his knees and beg forgiveness for betraying his best friend.

Ashley pulled the knitted afghan up to her chin and blinked hard, fighting the sleep that threatened to take over the rest of her day. Matt slipped into the living room, carrying her laptop, and closed the door most of the way. If someone needed something, they'd be able to hear through the crack, but they'd also have privacy.

"Are you sure you wouldn't be more comfortable in bed?"

"If I fall asleep now, my sleep schedule will be thrown completely off. Besides, I don't want to be alone right now. Please." Fighting the need to reach for his hand, she gripped the blanket until her knuckles were white. "Will you sit with me for a while?"

He glanced back toward the door, but finally nodded, settling onto the floor. With his back against the couch and legs stretched out, he set the computer on his knees and flipped it open.

"What else did the chief say?" She'd lost all her energy as soon as the police arrived, and he'd insisted on taking her to lie down once they'd confirmed that the shooter had vanished.

"Not much. He got kind of twitchy when I mentioned Miranda, and he said he hasn't found out anything about her disappearance. But it's pretty clear that he's worried about her."

"Did he have any idea who might have taken her?" A yawn caught her off guard, and she covered her mouth with a pale hand.

"No." He bent over the keyboard, using two fingers to tap out an email. "And he said he'd send the squad car around an extra three or four times a day."

She bit her lip to hold back a sarcastic comment. The chief was doing everything he could with the resources he had.

"Who are you writing?"

"My buddy Vince. He retired from navy intelligence a few years ago, but he's a wiz at finding out stuff online. Just asking him to look into Ithyka Inc. to find out who owns it, and what they might be doing with the bar."

He punched the keys like the keyboard had been behind the shooting, the sound echoing in the empty room.

"Where are the kids?"

"Playing in the kitchen."

She pushed an elbow under her and rolled to sit up. "I can go into the kitchen or my office so they can play in here."

Without looking up from the screen, he hooked her arm out from under her, sending her flat against the pillows stacked along the armrest. "They're fine. Lil is watching them. You've had a rough morning, so just relax for a few hours."

He went back to his typing, and she stared at the white popcorn ceiling, finding animals in the unusual shapes. When he finally hit Send, he set the computer aside and turned his whole body so he could look at her.

"Why do you always do that?"

"Do what?"

His eyes narrowed and he leaned toward her. "Try to be strong for everyone else but never let yourself off the hook for more than a minute."

Flames licked up her neck until her face burned all the way to her hairline. This was not a conversation she wanted to have with the man she'd just broken down in front of. But his gaze didn't waver.

How much of her soul could he see when he looked at her like that?

Only when she focused back on the cow chatting with the cat near the far corner of the ceiling could she respond. "I'm sorry about earlier. I don't usually do that."

His hand wrapped all the way around her forearm, prodding her to look back at him. "That's what I mean. Why are you so worried about not being strong in front of me?"

"You don't understand."

"Help me, then."

With a wrinkled nose, she flopped onto her side. "I'm not sure I can. You've never been… No one has ever taken advantage of your trust."

Something akin to pain flickered in his eyes and was gone as fast as it came. "Go on."

She'd only ever told one man about this part of her life, and then she'd had to. Tristan wouldn't have taken another excuse about a car accident when her car was in perfect shape.

"I was twenty, and I thought he was perfect. His name was Paul, and he said he loved me. He didn't."

In that moment his jaw could have cut granite as he ground his molars together. If he knew what was coming, why was he making her rehash that horrible time?

"You know the rest."

"No. I don't." He tipped his chin to rest on his chest, his fists on his outstretched legs. "I mean, I can fill in what Paul did, but I don't know how you got out of that relationship or why that makes you think that you have to be strong all the time."

"I tried to end it a few times." Her voice wobbled on her last word, and she cleared her throat to steady it. "Right after he hit me the first time, I told him it was over—told him never to call me again."

"And he begged for your forgiveness."

Her mouth suddenly turned into Death Valley, and she swallowed several times to no end. "The first time. After that, he quit apologizing. I tried to get a new apartment off campus, but he tracked me down. I got a dog, and Paul just beat him into submission."

By this point Matt's hands shook as he pressed a gentle palm to her arm. "I'm so sorry. No one should ever have to live through that. How long were you with him?"

"After the abuse started? Almost six months." His eyes asked the question that he really wanted to know, and she steeled herself to admit the truth. "It was Tristan who ended it. When I told him what Paul had done, he grabbed Zach and flew up to school—probably from somewhere overseas—so they could have a 'talk' with Paul." She accentuated the word *talk* with air quotes, even though Matt obviously knew what had happened.

"Did you ever see Paul again?"

"Across campus later that semester. He saw me, too, but then he turned and ran."

All of his features pinched tightly just before he

scrubbed his hands over his face, and she could make out only part of what he said. It sounded like "And why Tristan didn't bring *me* along for this talk, I'd like to know...."

"He transferred after that. I never saw him again."

He let his hands drop to his lap and studied them as he asked, "Were you already working on your degree in social work by that point?"

"Yes. I had been planning to go to work for the Department of Child Services, but after Paul... Well, after that, I realized there were a lot of adult victims, too, and maybe I could help them." The stinging started in the back of her eyes, and she had to bury her face in one of the pillows to keep her tears at bay.

"Is that when you decided that you had to be strong for everyone else?"

Wasn't it clear? Couldn't he see what had happened?

Apparently not. He was going to make her say the whole terrible truth aloud. What she'd never admitted to anyone in the world.

She'd never told a soul for fear that they'd take this and use it against her. But Matt would keep it safe. He knew how to protect her—and her secrets.

The words tumbled out with a slow sigh. "If I'd been strong back then, maybe I could have gotten myself out of the relationship on my own. Instead, I had to be rescued by my big brother. I was so weak that I couldn't stand up for myself. Someone else had to fight my battle."

"But that's what big brothers are for. You know that Tristan would do it again in a heartbeat. So would I. If you'd asked me, I'd have come running."

"That's just it. He would do it again. But he shouldn't have had to. It was my problem, and I should have been able to take care of it. Besides, what if Paul hadn't been a coward? What if a few choice words from Tristan hadn't made him run with his tail between his legs? What if the confrontation had ended with *Tristan* hurt, instead of Paul? Every time I let someone else fight my battles, I put them in danger."

"But Tristan is trained to defend himself. He can handle anyone."

"That's not the point. I need to be able to stand up for myself on my own." He opened his mouth to argue the point, but she held up her hand. "It's okay if you don't understand, but this is all I have. I refuse to be the woman I was. Please don't try to take that away from me."

His eyes turned sad, the corners of his mouth drooping. "I am sorry, Ashley. I wish that I could take that pain, those memories away from you."

"And then what? You'd have terrible memories of your own?"

"I've already got plenty of those."

She snapped her head in his direction, pushing herself up. With crossed legs pulled under her, she hugged a pillow to her chest and leaned forward. "What do you mean?"

He pursed his lips and looked up at the ceiling as he let out a slow breath. "Nothing really."

"I'm not letting you off the hook that easily, Waterstone." She leaned over the edge of the couch until her face was just inches from his. "What do you mean you have bad memories?"

The muscles in his forearm twitched as he leaned back on his hand, pulling his T-shirt tight across his chest and shoulders. The defined muscles couldn't hide under the jersey fabric, and she had to lift her gaze several times before she could hold eye contact.

He was trying to distract her, and it was working.

Fighting the urge, she stared hard at him. After several

seconds of silence, his gaze flicked away and he nodded in defeat. "I've never told this to a soul."

Ashley leaned forward, dangerously close to falling off the couch as her hair fell in front of her face.

So they had something in common. "Not even Tristan?"

"No. There was never time for it to come up during BUD/S, and after that it felt like it was too late to talk about that kind of stuff." He pressed his thumb to his chin, still not meeting her gaze.

"What kind of stuff?"

"You know. Being hit by the person who is supposed to take care of you. Showing up to school with black eyes and having to lie to your teachers and social worker about being clumsy when they actually ask what happened. Telling yourself someday you'd be strong enough that you'd never let anyone else hit you, but knowing that for now, you've got nothing to look forward to other than leaving one abusive foster father behind and finding a bigger, meaner man at the next home."

He took a breath, and she wanted to say something, but couldn't choke anything but the narrowest stream of air past the lump in her throat.

"Man, I hated all three of those guys. Paid to take in strays, but they just spent the money on booze, which made them meaner. When I was fourteen, I was the oldest and biggest kid in the house, and Lord knows I wasn't going to let that man beat on one of the littler ones.

"Funny how in the moment, you swear to yourself that you'll do anything to make sure that belt never hits you again. But the first time he swings a fist at the towheaded six-year-old, you find yourself in his way, ready to stand there until the kid can fight for himself."

His voice never wavered during the story; his eyes never left the seashore painting on the far wall.

She reached for his shoulder and then pulled her hand back, leaned in and then retreated, not knowing what response he'd appreciate. She'd thought her situation was bad, but this was nearly unbelievable.

When it was clear he wasn't going to speak again, she said, "How did you ever become a SEAL?"

He blinked at her as though he'd forgotten she was even there, the corner of his mouth raising. "I got a new case-worker just before I turned fifteen. Good thing, too, because I was planning to run away on my birthday. Mr. Crawford pulled me out and put me in a home that he said had had some success with 'trouble' cases like mine. I didn't know I was the problem, but I guess after a life-time of foster dads who hit before talking, every time, I had some attitude issues.

"Mr. and Mrs. Belkin owned a farm in Iowa, and as soon as I got to their place, they put me to work. They only had two rules. Go to church every Sunday, and don't talk back while doing your chores."

The smile that split his face could have blinded an as-tronaut. "Doing your chores wasn't even a rule. It was just expected.

"Mr. Belkin was in the navy during Korea, and he was the one that first suggested a kid with my particular skill set might be able to make a career of the teams."

"And what skill set was that exactly?"

His shoulders shook in silent laughter. "I guess some-one who had been in a few fights and wasn't afraid to face down a bully. I could swim a fair bit, too."

She rubbed the corner of her eye, surprised to find it damp. "Where are the Belkins now? Still helping trou-bled teens?"

His smile dimmed. "They passed away right after I joined the navy. Never got to see me get my trident pin when I made the teams, but I think they'd be proud of the man I've become."

"I'm sure of it." She didn't hold back when the urge to touch him swept her again, and his shoulder muscles twitched several times beneath her fingers.

"You know, it was Mrs. Belkin who first made me memorize that verse that we read yesterday morning—that God's strength is made perfect in our weakness. She said weakness wasn't a sin—in fact, it could be used in my favor. But it wasn't until I was on a rescue mission in Africa a few years ago that I got what she meant."

When had this conversation turned back to her strength and weakness? Because she was sure that was what he was getting at. There was no mistaking his meaning.

His gaze returned to the painting, and he was lost in memory before she could steer their conversation to safer ground.

"Tristan, Zach and I were supposed to extract an American being held hostage. A simple snatch and run. But when we got inside the hotel where she was being kept, everything went wrong. By the time we got to her, there was a tango using her as a human shield."

She assumed that a tango was a terrorist, but couldn't interrupt his story to confirm. With baited breath, she waited for the woman's fate.

"We'd trained for a scenario like that for years, and Zach is a dead-on marksman, but there wasn't a clear shot from any angle. Just when we thought we'd have to let the tango leave with her, she fainted. Out cold." He closed his eyes, his head falling to his shoulder. "Her dead weight caught the tango off guard, and he dropped her, giving us three clean shots."

"So when someone's weak there will always be three SEALs ready to take out the bad guy?"

He shrugged, pushing himself to a standing position. "I was thinking more along the lines that if she'd insisted on being strong all the time, we'd never have been able to rescue her." He leaned forward to press a kiss on her forehead, then walked away.

TWELVE

Matt fell into the only empty chair around the kitchen table, his heart still pounding and head spinning. He'd never talked so much in his entire life, especially not about his own life.

"Do you want the rest of my pie, Mr. Matt?" Greta, seated next to him, pushed her half-eaten piece of pie at him. "Sorry. I ate all the ice cream." She hissed through the gap where one of her front teeth had fallen out.

The little girl kept her fingers curled around the edge of her plate, waiting for him to turn down her offer. So when he shook his head, she snatched it back and ate the last bit in three quick bites. "You eat like my friends." He chuckled and ruffled her hair.

"Why's that?"

"Quit bothering Mr. Matt, Greta. It's time to brush your teeth and get ready for bed." The little girl batted her blue eyes—so like Ashley's—at her mom.

"But I'm not bothering him." She turned to him, a crumb still stuck to her chin. "Am I?"

"Never. But you should do what your mom says."

She shrugged, and even through the thick sweatshirt, her shoulders poked out. "Good night, Mr. Matt." Leaning over to him, she pressed a kiss to cheek, her arms wrapping around her neck. "Thanks for not eating my pie."

He patted her back and swallowed the lump in his throat as she scurried after her mom and the other three kids.

First Julio's midnight juice run and now a curly-headed five-year-old with a thing for pie. He'd never felt so needed and so helpless at the same time.

The letter-writing lunatic wasn't just threatening Ashley, who he hoped was finally sleeping on the couch. He put all of these kids—and the kids that would someday come into the house—in jeopardy.

Matt raked his hands down his face and stared toward the refrigerator without really seeing it. The calluses on his hands scratched his chin, an instant reminder of the difference between his life and Ashley's. She belonged here, caring for innocents. He didn't—not once he'd taken measures to make certain they were safe.

He belonged out there with his team, saving people with names he didn't always know, not next to little girls who made him ache for a family of his own. Ashley deserved to have a family, and despite her history, she'd find it. She'd find a man who could settle down with her and provide for her and take care of the women and children who came to stay at Lil's Place.

And that man wasn't him.

He couldn't stay here forever. He couldn't risk Ashley's heart any more than he already had.

She was clean houses and security systems.

He was explosives and dead-of-the-night rescue missions.

He had no right thinking about her as more than a promise to Tristan. Even if every time he closed his eyes he smelled that citrus shampoo and felt the warmth of her breath on his neck.

She was a mission. She had to be only a mission.

One he hadn't been able to complete—yet.

His phone burst to life, shaking in his pocket and beeping low and even. He snatched it and pressed it to his ear.

"Waterstone."

"Matt, it's Vince."

He let out a quick breath. At least it wasn't Tristan calling to check in again. "What'd you find out?"

It sounded like Vince shuffled some papers on the other end of the line. "Looked into the company you asked about, Ithyka."

"Did you find the owner?"

"Not yet. Ithyka is a subproperty of another corporation, which actually belongs to a conglomerate. And all of them seem to be front companies. They have lots of post office boxes but no actual addresses."

Matt kept his voice low, despite the unsettling news. "But I was there. At the Infinity bar. It has an address."

"Sure. The companies own plenty of property, but the companies themselves don't seem to have owners, and the management is more phantom than human."

"Who are these people?" Matt rubbed the curls on top of his head, scratching all the way to his ear and back. If he pressed hard enough, maybe he could stimulate an idea that explained this whole thing.

How was Miranda connected to Joy? And why was someone willing to kidnap her and terrorize Ashley to get to the girl?

Whoever it was, this wasn't their first rodeo. They'd covered their tracks, sent trained thugs and kept their identity hidden from the local police for a while now. That wasn't by accident.

"I don't know, man. I'll keep looking," Vince said.

"Thanks. Did you find out anything else?"

"One thing. I found three other properties within a twenty-mile radius of the Infinity that are owned by other companies in the conglomerate, and all three of them had fairly recent building permits through the city."

"How recent?"

"Umm…" Vince clicked away on a keyboard. "Within the last year or so."

He strummed heavy fingers on the table, rattling the plate that Greta had left behind. "Was there a building permit for the Infinity?"

More typing on the other end of the line as he pushed his chair back from the table and began pacing the confines of the small kitchen.

"Yes. A little over a year ago."

"Can you tell what kind of permit it was or if the construction was ever completed?"

"Sorry. All I can tell you is that the one outside the city limits was a permit to add a basement to a single-story building. I haven't gotten into the files for the other permits yet."

"Did you say the permit was to install a basement? In a preexisting structure?" He couldn't keep the incredulity from his voice. "That's ridiculous."

"Don't know what to tell you, man. It's right there on the permit."

Four buildings within forty miles of each other. All with building permits, and at least one basement. Except, the construction on the Infinity hadn't reopened the bar. It was still closed. Had it gotten a basement, too?

"Will you text me those other addresses?"

"Of course."

"And you'll keep looking for a name to go along with these?" He hated the way his voice rose, matching the desperation that threatened to rise like bile from his stomach.

He had to figure this out. The warning shot had been just that. A warning. The next shot would meet its mark.

"Sure thing."

Matt turned off his phone, circling the room with even steps and zero pain in his leg.

By the next morning, he hated his healed leg. At least when it burned every time he moved, he had a good excuse for not sleeping well. This time, he'd lost a night of sleep to images of Ashley's face as her car window shattered.

Long before the sun rose, he slipped off his cot and pulled on his sweats and tennis shoes. If his leg really was better, a jog might make him more pleasant for the rest of the day.

And he knew just where his run would take him.

One of the addresses from Vince was only a little over two miles away. He could get there and back in about twenty minutes on a regular day. It'd probably take him twice that after a few weeks of limited PT.

The night had turned the hallway eerily silent as he crept toward the muted beam of the night-light. Every room was still, but he hovered outside Ashley's door, ear pressed to the wooden panel.

He raised a hand to knock, but stopped short.

She'd insist on going with him, but she was safer here than out in the open. Besides, he could make it there and back before she even woke up. She'd argue about it, but in the end it was best for him to go alone. Only God knew what was waiting at the building he was heading to.

Creeping to the front door, he punched in the security code that allowed him to open the door, then immediately reengaged the system once the door shut behind him.

The moon shone big and bright in the morning sky, showing him the exact path toward his destination. After three slow steps, he picked up speed, his legs going slower at first and then gaining momentum. Nowhere near the five-minute-mile pace he'd had in BUD/S, but decent, given the injury and time off.

In short order the rhythm of his feet pounding on the deserted streets set his mind on things he didn't want to think about anymore.

Like how he knew it was best for Ashley and for him to go their separate ways, but it didn't make the ache in the pit of his stomach any easier to deal with. Like how in less than a week he'd gotten so used to having her around that going back to San Diego without her was going to be miserable.

Like the way he'd do anything so she'd never again have to carry the fear he'd seen when she was shot at.

"God, what am I going to do about her?" The words floated away on the morning breeze before he realized he'd even spoken them aloud. He'd been doing a lot of recon and a lot of pining for Ashley. But he sure hadn't been doing much praying about the situation.

Streetlights began to blink off as the sun rose to his back, his sweatshirt becoming almost too much. He stopped next to a green sedan parked at the curb to take it off. His breath came in quick spurts, and he bent to rest his hands on his knees.

Man, he was out of shape. He hadn't realized how far of a setback three weeks without training would cause.

As he sucked in deep breaths, head nearly between his knees, he did what he should have done all along. He'd wanted to be strong for her, but she needed more than his strength.

"God, I'm a little lost here. I've been trying so hard to be what Ashley needs right now and then worrying that I can't be what she needs for the future. I know that all she really needs is Your strength. Would You give us both an extra shot of it today?"

The burst of energy that followed sent him sailing down the road until he arrived on the street that Vince had indicated. Unlike the neighborhood surrounding the Infinity, the buildings in this area were immaculate. Warehouse after white warehouse rose along the industrial road about twenty feet beyond chain link fences. There was no sign of rust or even everyday wear.

Someone cared about these buildings. But whatever was in them didn't warrant an intense security system. The fences were only eight feet and several sported cuts through the wire where would-be thieves had probably broken in.

All were unremarkable. Except for the fence surrounding the building at the end of the street. It rose at least two feet higher than the others, and a spiral of barbed wire followed the whole length of the barrier. Several cuts through the wire on the far side of the property had been patched with welded iron tourniquets.

He never slowed his pace as he turned the corner past the address in question until he reached an alley and ducked in there. He hunched into the darkness, scanning the street for any sign of early-morning activity. After ten minutes of nothing, he slipped back into the street and hurried to the fence.

The only entrance to the fence was on the backside of the building, and it was chained with industrial-strength links and a combination lock.

What he wouldn't give for half a block of C-4.

His only option was up and over.

Untying his sweatshirt from his waist, he shimmied up the fence and tossed his jacket so it covered the barbed-wire roll. With a quick hop, he was on the other side, and he lowered himself to the ground, dropping the last three feet into an instinctive squat and pulling his sweatshirt with him. He waited for any indication that he'd been spotted, but all was still, so he bolted for the side of the building.

Through a single window in the top half of the door, he peered into the wide room. It was basically a cement slab with four walls. No equipment or office. No place to sit or boxes stacked as storage.

That barbed wire was completely superfluous if this was all there was to it.

There had to be more. Maybe this place had a basement, too.

He slipped around the perimeter of the building, following the long side until he reached a metal door, similar to the cellar entrance at the Belkins' farm. The handle had a latch to hold it in place, but no lock.

As he pulled the oversize door open, the hinges squeaked in protest. He stopped moving and held his breath, eyes darting around the compound in the growing dawn.

Hugging the cinder block wall all the way to the end of the stairwell, he inched into the basement. The narrow opening emptied into a nearly pitch-black hallway, and he blinked several times, trying to get his eyes to adjust.

It didn't do much good, so he closed his eyes and held his breath, waiting for any other sound. No voices or breathing. No shuffles or scurries. It was deserted.

Taking a quick breath, he nearly gagged, eyes gushing with unshed tears. It smelled of human waste and unwashed bodies, just like the South American prison he'd once had the misfortune to be sent to on a mission.

Blinking several times and breathing through his mouth, he pressed forward. Someone had been held underground long enough to make the place reek. Probably more than one someone.

Using his fingertips to navigate the hallway, he found a large metal door, pushed open all the way to the adjacent wall. Above the cold metal handle were two bolt latches. And their matching openings were installed on the opposite side of the door frame.

He felt his way into the dark room, his hands running along the wall at shoulder height until he ran into the rusted metal of a chain. It hung from the wall, and he followed it all the way to the opposite corner where a manacle lay in a pool of something that did not smell like water.

He squatted in the corner, trying to understand what had happened here. Clearly at some point, this place had held people against their will. People like…Joy? And whoever would do something like this didn't have an ounce of respect for life. No wonder Miranda had told Ashley that Joy needed to get out of town, where no one would find her. Whoever this man was, he wasn't afraid of taking a life.

And Ashley was on his chopping block.

He had to get back to her immediately.

Just as he stepped into the hallway, the heavy metal door creaked again, followed by two sets of footsteps down the stairs.

He wasn't alone anymore.

THIRTEEN

Matt stole a quick breath, sliding back into the room and praying that the new arrivals wouldn't hear him. Every muscle in his body tensed, and he leaned forward on his toes, still within the protection of the cage.

"Where's the light switch?" One of the men stubbed his toe on the other side of the wall and let out a string of curses that would have put any of the SEALs to shame.

The other man offered a different swear in response to the pungent odor.

Bright couple of guys, these two. He could take them out in about four seconds flat, even in the dark. But what if they had useful information? Clearly someone had sent them here. They made enough ruckus to rival the noise on the deck of an aircraft carrier, so they either didn't know he was there or they didn't care.

He'd stake another leg injury that it was the former.

A dim light flickered at the foot of the stairs, and he snuck three sharp breaths as he loosened his fists and wiggled his fingers.

"So what did he say?"

The guy with the stubbed toe sighed like he'd been forced to work with the village idiot. "The boss said we're supposed to get the rooms ready. They're transferring a bunch of them tomorrow."

"Why're they bringing them here?" Maybe that guy really was the village idiot.

After a long pause, the one with the minor limp sighed. "Because, they're getting inspected. Because the feds are checking out the other place." He stomped off to the far end of the hall, his companion dragging his feet in pursuit.

They were transferring a shipment into a basement with shackles and the distinct smell of dirty humans. It didn't take a genius to figure out exactly what that "shipment" contained. Someone was keeping people in this basement. And probably in three others.

How had he missed it when they searched the Infinity? He'd joked about finding a picture of Joy when they searched the bar, but if they'd thought to look for a basement, they might have found equally clear personal markers—if she'd been there, Joy's DNA would be there, too.

Ashley had said she'd been bruised from her wrist to her elbow and that someone had done a number on her. If Joy had fought the handcuff at the end of the chain, it would have easily done that kind of damage.

Human traffickers with no respect for life wanted the girl back. And they'd kill Ashley to get to her. But why? Did they think her broken English could reveal too much about their operation to the authorities?

"What about that Asian girl? The boss ever get her back?"

"Not yet."

Chains clanked and a hose sprayed down one of the far cells, covering most of what was said, but it was clear that someone wasn't happy with Joy's disappearance.

"He find a buyer?"

"Stupid idiot. He's had a buyer. For the last two weeks. That's why he needs her back."

Bile rose in the back of Matt's throat, and he swallowed it quickly before he gagged on it, giving away his position. Buyers and sellers. They spoke like they were selling livestock, not people.

For a moment he let himself believe he was wrong. It wasn't humans being held here. It wasn't even animals. He had imagined the whole thing.

"What are they going to do with her when they find her?"

Except he hadn't.

"Shut up." The sound of flesh hitting flesh was unmistakable. "Don't be stupid. You know the boss won't stand for anyone to steal from him."

Especially a petite, blonde shelter director. He didn't have to say it aloud for it to be true. If the boss was trying to deliver Joy to a wealthy buyer, every day meant more trouble and probably more pressure to get her back. More pressure to force *Ashley* to give her back.

Time was running out. He had to get back to Lil's to warn her and make sure that Joy was still safely hidden.

With no idea how long the other two men would stick around, he didn't have many options. He had to reveal himself and pray that they didn't have more buddies waiting outside. Taking a long, slow breath, he closed his eyes and clenched his fists. A short run may have winded him, but his injury couldn't take away the years of training drilled into him by the toughest bunch of SEAL instructors to ever walk the earth.

He waited for the hose to turn on again before peeking into the hallway. The dim light was his only ally. One of the men stood at the far end, spraying the second stall. The other was walking straight toward him, his head turned as he yelled at his friend.

"Where'd you say the other one was?" His voice bounced off the cement as he headed for the base of the stairs.

Matt sank to his haunches, his movements noiseless, and he waited.

Keeping an eye on the first man's shadow, he shot a hand out to yank on the man's wrist, dodging as the giant crashed to the floor, disoriented and clearly shocked.

"What the—"

Matt effectively cut the man's words at the quick with a swift elbow to the chest before wrapping his arm around the meaty neck, locking his hold in place with his opposite wrist. The man thrashed about, like a marlin on the end of a line, his hands alternately slapping the cement floor and clawing at the arm that was cutting off his air supply.

"Jack? Where did you go? Where's the other hose?" Footsteps echoed from the far end of the hallway.

They were about to have company.

Matt loosened his grip on Jack, who had passed out and now laid motionless, save for the shallow rise and fall of his chest. He'd have a raging headache when he woke up, but that would be a little while yet.

Jack's partner stalked right past the first cell, so that Matt had to chase him up the stairs, tackling him at the knees. The man fell so hard that he didn't even have time to hold out his hands to stop the fall. His face cracked against the cement with a sharp report.

That was going to leave a nasty bruise, but he couldn't afford to have the man alerting his boss until Ashley was safe.

With a shudder, Matt pushed himself to his knees and dragged the second unconscious man back down the stairs.

Then he hustled past the four cells on each side of the hall to the garden hose. With swift fingers he unscrewed the metal end attached to the spigot, then took it back to the two limp forms. A few creative knots was all it took to secure them to the chains on the wall, at least for the time being.

The knots wouldn't hold for long, but it might slow them down long enough to give the police a chance to get there. Maybe they hadn't actually done anything illegal in the basement, but guys like this usually had rap sheets a mile long, and, if he was lucky, an outstanding warrant or two.

Now he had to get back to Ashley. There was no telling what their boss had in store for her, as long as she hid Joy.

Ashley jerked awake, the sound of a door closing drawing her from a fitful sleep. Slipping on her jeans and a sweater, she tiptoed into the empty hallway. Careful to avoid the hardwood slat that always creaked when stepped on, she scurried toward the front door.

When she got there, her stomach flipped and twirled as fast as the flashing light of the alarm system keypad.

Someone had just reset it, and it didn't take a gumshoe to figure out who. The laundry room door stood wide-open; Matt's cot was empty and his blankets were folded neatly on the foot of the bed. Apparently navy habits died hard, even on leave.

How could he leave her alone? Of course she could take care of things herself, but that didn't make it okay that he'd suddenly decided to take off without so much as a word about it. They'd been shot at, threatened and assaulted. And he thought it was a good time to waltz off without telling her?

Taking a deep breath and wrapping her arms around her stomach, she tried to talk herself out of her own insanity.

"He's probably just checking around the house." Her whisper barely carried to her own ears let alone down the corridor. "I don't need him here with me every single second, and anyway, he'll be back in a minute."

He didn't come back in a minute. In fact, after three minutes ticked out in agonizing seconds on the grandfather clock, the only change was the uneasiness brewing in her stomach.

What if the noise that had woken her wasn't Matt leaving but someone entering? Or what if Matt had gone out and had been injured again?

Fear built upon fear, and she squeezed her eyes tight against the sudden desire to crumble to the floor and hide from everything that this day represented.

But she had to be strong. If she couldn't be strong with Matt gone, she'd never be able to be strong with him there. She could face this morning, this day, without him. Wherever he was.

She snuck up to the door and brushed the curtain aside just enough to scope out the front yard.

Empty.

"God, I'm being so silly. Give me a peaceful heart today."

She couldn't quite produce a true smile as she turned toward her office, but the churning in her stomach had slowed. Settled into her desk chair, she picked up her address book, automatically flipping through the pages until she reached the last, and punched in the number Tristan had written in years before. His voice mail picked up after half a ring.

"This is Matt Waterstone. Sorry I missed you. Leave a message, and I'll call you back."

After the phone beeped, she stared at it for several long

seconds before hanging up. No use unloading her ridiculous worries on him. He'd be back shortly.

But maybe she could do a little investigating while she was alone. After a quick glance at the clock on the wall, she punched a different number into the keypad.

"Chief Donal."

"This is Ashley Sawyer."

"Ashley." He gave her name two extra syllables, like his tongue was too heavy to annunciate. "What can I do for you…at seven-thirty this morning?"

A thick strand of hair fell into her face, and she brushed it behind her ear. "Have you heard anything lately?"

"Anything about what?"

The hair escaped again, and she ran her fingers through it to put it back into place. "You know what. My shattered windshield. The brick that someone threw through my window. The notes. Miranda's disappearance. The gunshot that sailed right past my head and blew out my car's window. Feel free to pick any of them."

He cleared his throat, and she could picture him loosening his tie. "I'm afraid there isn't much to say."

"On which one?"

"All of them."

Her head fell forward into her hand, propped up by an elbow on the desk. The wayward strand fell, too, and she blew a frustrated sigh out of the corner of her mouth, sending the hair flying. "You must have something. Anything." The pitch of her voice rose, and she cringed. The desperation was evident, and she had to fight it. Had to stay strong. "Please. Give me something."

He shuffled some papers, the gentle scratching crystal clear over the phone line. "Let's see. The notes didn't have any prints on them. Not even the one that was attached to the brick that went through your front window." As he continued looking, he whistled under his breath and she held hers.

There had to be something that would give them a clue, because the next shot might miss her again but hit one of the others. She pressed the heel of her palm into her eye, only adding to the pressure building there.

Giving up Joy wasn't the answer. It wasn't even an option. She'd die before she'd give the wounded, haunted girl back to this lunatic. Her huge almond-shaped eyes had stared, never blinking, as she trembled just inside the back door. She'd bitten her lip and nodded at Miranda's prodding, speaking rarely and even then, never above a whisper. Except for when they prompted her to hold her arms out so they could check her over, not once had she pulled her arms from where they were wrapped around her body. She had barely even flinched when they'd gently prodded her arms for broken bones beneath that sea of bruises.

This was all because Joy had stumbled into her home. Joy was the link to the midnight blue Suburban and the man behind it all.

So maybe they should be trying to find out more about her.

"Chief! Can you look into something for me?"

"What kind of something?"

She rubbed her forehead, inadvertently pulling that wayward strand of hair back into her face. Blowing it away again, she leaned over to reach her filing cabinet beside the desk. As her fingers skimmed the file names, she chewed her lip, trying to find the right words. "I think that my troubles are all related to an abused woman we had at the house a few weeks ago."

"Why is this the first I'm hearing of it?" His voice rose an octave. "Who is she?"

"I'm not quite sure, but she was in serious trouble."

"What kind of trouble?"

"She was beat up pretty bad, mostly on her arms."

"Self-defense?"

Ashley finally found the file she had been looking for and pulled it from the cabinet, laying it open on her desk. "I don't think so. The bruises went all the way around her arms, like they'd been made by a hand circling the whole way."

He sighed as though she was the bane of his existence. "Where is she now?"

It would be so easy to just hand the whole thing over to the chief, to tell him where the girl was hidden. But what if he let it slip to the wrong person? She couldn't risk the information about Joy's location getting out to anyone. She just needed to know more about her. Maybe they could figure out who was after her if they knew more about who she was.

"Could you maybe find out who she is first?"

"First?" She could picture his face turning red, the vein in his forehead throbbing as his agitation grew. "How about first you tell me where I can find her?"

"I can't. I just need to know if there are any missing person reports out there for her. Could you just check to see if there are reports within a five-hundred-mile radius for someone matching her description?"

"Five hundred miles? Are you kidding me? That's all the way into Nevada, which means getting the feds involved, which would be a whole 'nother mess."

She steepled her hands in front of her mouth, scanning the file for any bit of information she might have overlooked. What could be useful? What would point to Joy's true identity?

Ignoring the chief's qualms, she dove into the description he should search for. "She's of Asian heritage. Between the ages of sixteen and twenty."

"Whoa. Hold up right there, Ms. Sawyer. If she was underage, you should have called Child Protective Services immediately."

A flood of heat washed over her face. She hadn't meant to admit that she thought the girl could be so young, but if he agreed to search for a missing person, he had to consider all possibilities.

"She said she was eighteen."

"Did she have any sort of identification?" he asked, pressing the point.

"None."

"So you just took her word for it that she was of age?" Sarcasm dripped from his words like honey from the comb. "Of course you did." By now the pulsing in his forehead was likely about to pop, but she didn't have anything to add that would soften the blow.

"She was in trouble. And she still is."

"Because the person you think is after you is actually after her." He didn't sound like he believed her at all.

She mouthed a prayer under her breath, asking for the right words, not even sure where to begin. "Chief, I know you're a busy man. And I know you have a small staff. Your office deserves more than you've got. But you're still here to serve and protect the citizens of Charity Way, right?"

He grumbled something that she'd never be able to repeat, but finally said, "I suppose."

"Well, I need your services right now. I need you to help protect me and the families at Lil's Place. You've followed up on every lead we've given you, right?"

His huff echoed over the line. "Of course." Now he was offended.

Good.

"Well, I'm giving you another lead. Follow up on Joy. You don't need to know where she is to figure out if anyone is missing her."

"I'll see if I can get someone on it this week."

Time to pull out the big guns. "What if finding out Joy's past will reveal what happened to Miranda? I'm sure the two are linked. Miranda was the one who brought her here."

He mumbled a few choice words through his hand and finished with a loud groan. "Fine. Give me her details again."

Ashley ran through the list of notes she'd taken on the girl. Height. Approximate weight. Even a description of the torn blue jeans and stained pink sweater she'd been wearing. After asking a few more questions, he hung up with a promise to check into any reports and even call a friend who worked across the state line.

She leaned back in her chair and crossed her arms, a smile creeping into place. It wasn't much, but she'd done something. She'd done as much as she could for the moment. Maybe it wouldn't pan out, but maybe the chief would uncover something that would blow the whole case wide open.

The three sharp reports on the door of her office made her jump, and she turned just as Benita poked her head in.

"I'm so sorry to bother you, Ashley, but it's Julio."

She stood and hurried across the floor to hold the other woman's shaking hand. "What is it?"

"He's running a terrible fever. It's over one hundred and one already." Benita's eyes clouded with concern; the features of her face pulled into a tight mask of her own pain.

"Did you give him something to bring it down?"

"We're all out. Meghan gave Greta the last of the fever reducer last week."

Ashley grabbed her purse as she stepped all the way into the hallway. "I'll run to the pharmacy right now and pick some up."

"Thank you."

Before ducking out the front door, she poked her head into Lil's room. The older woman sat in her rocking chair, her Bible open across her lap.

"I'm running to the store. I'll be right back."

"Is Matt going with you?"

She chewed on the corner of her lip. "I'm not sure where he is right now. But he'll probably be back soon."

Lil pushed a slipper-covered toe against the floor, the gentle rocking motion of the old wooden chair contrasting with the sudden tightening of the lines around her mouth. "Maybe you should wait until he gets back."

The thought was tempting. She could wait for him and hold his arm as they walked the eight blocks to the store. She could wait and be assured of safety.

But Julio couldn't wait.

This is what it meant to be strong for her girls. Going outside even when she wanted nothing more than to curl up and wait for someone else to face the unknown.

"I'll be back in a few minutes. Don't worry about me." Her voice caught on the last word, and she cleared her throat to cover her own fear before offering a solid smile. "I'll be fine."

She disengaged the alarm system, but didn't open the door until she'd inspected the yard for any intruders. The pitch in her stomach had less to do with what she thought she might find there and far too much with hoping to see signs of Matt returning.

The yard was as untouched and empty as it had been

almost an hour earlier. And the raised hair on her arms was from the morning chill. Right?

She dipped her hand into the outside pocket of her purse, her fingers wrapping around the thin metal tube of pepper spray.

Taking a deep breath, she opened the door and slipped outside.

Just as she turned to lock the dead bolt behind her, an arm twisted around her waist while another one wrapped around her throat. She started to scream, but it was cut off as abruptly as it began. The arm around her waist moved to cover her mouth, and the one around her neck tightened, cutting off her supply of air as everything went black.

FOURTEEN

As he rounded the corner two blocks from Lil's at a dead run, Matt pushed everything but Ashley's welfare out of his mind. His ears rang with the pounding of blood, his muscles burning.

A scream pierced through his consciousness. It was high-pitched, filled with fear and cut off quickly.

Ashley.

He knew it in his heart even before he saw her blond hair disappear into the backseat of a painfully familiar midnight-blue SUV. Before he heard the back doors slam and the tires squeal against the pavement.

Pressing his body for every ounce of strength left, he reached his truck and jumped in.

Like a fool, he'd left his keys inside, so he made quick work of hot-wiring the engine, a skill he'd picked up from one of his foster brothers.

In six seconds flat he was flooring the old pickup after the abductors, swerving between lanes and sailing around morning commuters.

As his knuckles turned white around the steering wheel, he took three deep breaths. His eyes swept the roadways and every side street for any sign of the SUV.

Where had it disappeared to?

He'd been after it within moments. It couldn't have vanished so quickly. Not with Ashley in it.

He had to find her.

He had to save her.

But what if he couldn't?

Human traffickers had a vast underground system for moving their wares. He'd seen it before in places like Thailand, but it happened stateside, too. Women and kids disappeared and popped up hundreds of miles away, slaves to a system that made his head spin and his stomach roll.

What if he couldn't find her?

Pain shot through this chest, a band around his heart pulling taut. He kept both hands on the wheel as he flew through a yellow traffic light, despite the need to claw at his chest to relieve the pressure building there.

A flash of blue caught his eye, and he crossed three lanes of traffic to follow it before realizing it was a sports car. He spun again onto Main Street, not far from the police station. The colorful awnings of the town's tourist district taunted him with their cheerful appearance.

He'd lost her. He'd lost the woman he loved.

The knot in his stomach twisted so hard that he had to pull off into an alley so he could get out of his truck and wretch.

With one arm resting against the cement block wall of a building, he leaned over and emptied his stomach, his whole body shaking.

No mission, successful or not, had ever made him physically ill.

But this was so much more than a mission.

He pressed his shoulder into the wall, just needing something to lean on, a groan coming from deep inside as he wiped the back of his hand across his mouth.

How had this happened? How had he failed to protect

her as he was supposed to—as he wanted to? Why had he left her alone even for just an hour? He'd seen the kind of things these beasts did to humans. And now they had Ashley.

God had to give him the strength to get her back.

There wasn't any other option.

Jumping back into his truck, he pulled out of the alley and headed back to Lil's. More than likely the women there were still fine, but that didn't mean he was okay with leaving them unattended while he figured out his next step.

As he barreled toward the house, he punched a number into his phone, flicking it to the hands-free setting as he turned a corner on two wheels.

After four rings, the phone crackled to life. "This is Vince."

"It's Matt. I need—"

"Sorry I missed your call." Matt threw the truck into Park outside the house and grabbed his phone as he jumped out, running up the front walk as Vince's voice mail finished its outgoing message.

Before entering the house, Matt spoke softly into the phone. "This is Matt. I need whatever you've got. *Now.*"

He hung up and took two quick breaths, forcing his features to relax and his heart to slow to its regular pace before walking inside. His hands were rock-steady as he unlocked the dead bolt and stepped into a beehive of high-pitched terror.

"Matthew! Matthew, someone's taken Ashley." Lil grabbed his arm first, her weathered fingers cold and insistent as they pressed into his wrist.

Benita joined her at his other arm, not touching him, but staring up with pleading eyes. "She's gone. It's my fault! Julio's sick, and Ashley said she'd go to get medicine. I shouldn't have let her go! But she just stepped outside and then she was gone. We heard her start to scream, and I got to the window in time to see that there was a big blue SUV, and they pushed her into it."

"I know."

Both women looked stunned, and suddenly all of the chatter stopped, every eye settling on him. He raked a hand down his face, eyes pinched against the throbbing in his temples.

When he opened his eyes, Lil squinted at him, her frown creating wrinkles from her fluffy white hair to her loosening jowls. "But how?"

How could he explain that he'd seen the whole thing from more than a block away but had been unable to do anything about it?

The women began twittering among themselves when he didn't say anything right away, so he held up his hands to silence them. "I was just returning from a jog when I saw the same thing you did, Benita. I saw her get pushed into the back of the same blue Suburban that tried to run us off the road a few days ago." Several women gasped, but he kept going. "She's in trouble right now, but I promise you that I'm going to do whatever it takes to get her back."

"What can we do to help?" Lil's hand squeezed his.

Maybe she understood that he had to do this for himself more than for them.

"First, everyone needs to stay calm." The women nodded. "The men who kidnapped Ashley aren't really after her. They're after someone who came through here a couple weeks ago. If Ashley doesn't give them the information they need to find the girl they're looking for, they may come after one of you."

The soprano twittering resumed with gusto, but this time it was Lil who quieted them. "Ladies, please. Stay calm. We're all safe right now." She turned back to him. "What can we do?" she repeated.

He gave her a half smile, focused on all the things yet to be done. "Stay in one room. Why don't we set up the living room as a fort, and keep everyone in the same place. No one goes outside. No one stands by windows. Get the kids set up in there to watch a movie or play some games or something."

"For how long?" Benita's voice rose above the others. "And what about Julio?"

Matt wrinkled his forehead. "Stay put until Ashley's back. And why don't you take him into your room and keep him there for now so he doesn't spread whatever he has to the others?"

His phone let out a low chirp, vibrating in his pocket. "I'm going to need the kitchen to myself for a while. Can you take care of this, Lil? And maybe call a volunteer who could drop off something for Julio to bring down his fever."

"Certainly."

He caught her arm before she disappeared with the rest down the hallway. "If the phone rings, don't answer it. Just get me immediately."

She nodded slowly before continuing to herd the women toward the bedrooms, where they immediately began collecting their children and ushering them toward the living room.

He closed the kitchen door behind him as he took a call from an unregistered number. "This is Matt."

"Matteo!"

His stomach plunged through the floor. "Tristan." He paced the confines of the small room, the muscles in his shoulders twitching with every turn. "What's going on?"

"We touched down about an hour ago. Just going into

debriefing right now, but wanted to check on you and Ashley. She's not answering her phone."

"Welcome home." His voice felt heavier than the granite countertops lining the room.

Tristan laughed, his full-on belly laugh. "You don't sound happy to hear from me. But I'll forgive you because you're probably still ticked that you didn't get to go with us."

"Something like that." He took a deep breath and leaned over the counter, resting his forearms between the toaster and coffeemaker. "Listen, there's something I need to tell you."

I accidentally let your sister get kidnapped by a raging lunatic somewhere along the line, but it's okay because the real gut punch is that I fell in love with her, too. So, you know, I'll lay my own life down to rescue her.

It didn't quite have the right ring to it.

"Sure thing. I've got to jet. But put Ash on the phone real fast. I just want to say hi."

"She's not here."

He must have heard something in Matt's tone because Tristan, who never stopped moving, was suddenly completely silent, his shallow breathing the only indication he was still on the line for fifteen seconds. "Where is she?"

Dear God, he'd failed.

And this wasn't a failure he could hide. This one was going to stare him in the face, reminding him of his mistakes, for the rest of his life.

But it didn't change the truth. He had to tell Tristan.

"A girl came through the shelter a couple weeks ago, and Ashley didn't know it, but somehow she'd gotten away from human traffickers. Those guys have been looking for her, trying to get Ashley to turn her over. That's what the first threatening note was about—and all the notes and threats since."

He scrubbed his face with a flat palm, waiting for Tristan to say something. Anything. But he didn't.

"I went to go check out a building on our radar this morning. It was so early, and I swear, I thought she'd just stay home with the security alarm on. I was only going to be gone for an hour, and it was still dark when I left. And I couldn't take her with me to recon a building. But one of the kids got sick and needed some medicine."

He cleared his throat once, pushing down the lump in it. "I was a block away when I heard her scream. She must have been outside for five seconds, tops. They pushed her into the backseat of a transport vehicle and took off. I chased them, but they disappeared."

In that moment, Matt wished that Tristan had the same rage as his first foster dads. He could handle it if Tristan lashed out at him. In fact, he deserved it.

But the quiet, lethal voice that came over the phone was the opposite of wild, unfocused rage. "We'll be there in about eight hours. Have a plan in place."

"Yes, sir."

As he sank into a kitchen chair, he stared at the phone in his hand, as though it would tell him where Ashley was.

He had eight hours—seven if Tristan was driving—to find her. Eight hours to recon the area and follow up on every lead. Eight hours to put together a rescue mission that could not fail.

It took a never-say-die attitude to finish BUD/S training. It took hours in the gym and even more hours mentally preparing to drop in behind enemy lines or rescue hostages.

But no attitude or amount of strength would bring Ashley back right now.

Leaning his head back, he stared at the ceiling for several long seconds, spearing his fingers through his hair.

"All right, God. I get the irony. I've been telling Ashley it's okay to be weak, but I'm ready to pull my hair out right now. I've never felt so useless in my life. No intel. No direction. You're going to have to step in here. Please. *Please.*"

Ashley jerked her hand away from the goon who pulled at her arm. "Hold still," he growled as he slapped a handcuff around her wrist and attached the other side to a chain on the wall.

"Please don't." Her words vanished in the air, as useless as her cries for help had been ever since she'd come to on their drive away from Lil's.

"Get comfortable. The boss will be around later to see you." He pushed her arm, sending her flying across the room. She landed hard on a thin strip of cotton balls masquerading as a mattress at the same moment that he slammed her cell door closed. The threadbare fabric holding the flimsy puffs together scratched her elbows as she tried to soften the fall, sending fire up her arms.

As she tried to push herself up, the slack on her chain ran out, and she stumbled back to the floor, this time landing on her knees. Something wet and slimy coated her pants, and she rolled back onto the mattress. At least it was dry.

She rubbed her head with shaking hands, and flinched when her fingers found a bump over her right ear. Where someone had thumped her with the butt of a handgun when he'd decided she was making too much noise on the drive here.

It had felt more like she'd been shot, but since there was no blood and she was still alive, that wasn't the case.

The only light in the cement room came from the hallway visible through a one-foot, square window in the door, lined with bars. Of course, they'd blindfolded her on the way to the cell, so she hadn't seen the hallway. But she was, nonetheless, thankful for its light that left a small patch of hope on the floor.

Taking a deep breath, she pulled her knees up to her chest and pressed her forehead against them, trying to force her pulse to return to normal. It was a struggle, though, not to hyperventilate when she thought of how she had no one to blame for her current situation but herself.

If only this didn't make sense. If only this had happened out of the blue.

But she'd known it was coming. She'd known she was in danger, and she'd left the safety of the house.

Matt didn't know she was gone. Even if he'd realized by now, he didn't know where she'd been stashed.

She didn't even know where she was.

If she was going to get free, she'd have to do it herself. That thought, finally, was the one that stabilized her breathing and cleared her head. She knew how to be strong, even when she was scared. Now was the time to put that knowledge to use.

Giving her legs one more good squeeze, she stood and tugged on the chain. It clanked against the ground with finality, moving only an inch, its weight more than she'd imagined and certainly unbreakable.

Maybe the handcuff would release easier.

She held it into the stream of light and inspected it. It wasn't like a normal set of police handcuffs. It didn't have a lock and key release but rather a dead-bolt-type lock on the bottom side of her wrist. One little twist should release it.

It didn't.

It just made it tighter.

She tried again. Same result.

Her eyes burned, and she pressed her fingers against them. Tears still leaked out, turning the dirt on her hands sticky.

This wasn't right. There had to be a way out.

Taking a deep breath and opening her eyes, she spun to take inventory of the room, but three of the corners remained hidden in the shadows, including the one that seemed to hold the other end of the chain.

With baby steps she followed each link into the recesses. The far end of the chain connected to a ring that disappeared into the wall. Just like the prisons in old movies.

Another futile attempt.

She shook her head, refusing to give up.

It couldn't be hopeless.

The boss—whoever that was—would come for her at some point, and she'd be able to escape then.

She had to.

For Lil. For Benita, Meghan and Carmen. For all the abused women and kids that would come through Lil's door.

For Matt.

His face flashed on the backs of her eyelids, beaming smile, brilliantly blue eyes and wind-tossed curls. So handsome and so strong.

Why hadn't she listened to him?

She'd gotten herself into this mess. If she'd just listened she could be safe at home with him, surrounded by the people she cared about the most.

She'd been so stupid.

She yanked on the chain and it cracked against the floor.

"Don't do that." The insistent voice came through the

wall at her back, so she leaned toward it. "He—he doesn't like it when we make too much noise."

"Who doesn't like it?"

"The boss."

"Who are you?" Ashley held her breath.

"I'm no one. Just—just don't make too much noise." The woman's voice shook with each syllable, making her sound like a child.

Then again, Joy had been little more than a child.

"Please." Ashley tried again. Maybe this girl could help. Maybe they could escape together. Now that she knew she wasn't alone, leaving the other woman behind wasn't an option. "Why do we have to be quiet?"

"It doesn't matter. Just hush. He's coming."

Footsteps echoed in the hall, growing louder with each one until they stopped outside her door. The lock on the door unlatched, and it flew in. A megawatt flashlight swam across the floor until it shined directly into her face.

"Good afternoon, Ms. Sawyer. You have something that belongs to me."

She knew that voice.

FIFTEEN

Ashley lunged out of the spotlight, her eyes burning from its intensity. Holding a hand at her forehead to get a better view of her visitor, she scurried deeper into the shadows, but all she could make out was a tall silhouette with broad shoulders and shaggy hair hanging over his collar. Just as it had been the last time she'd seen him at the police station.

"Jimmy. Jimmy Swift." Her voice filled the room, bouncing from wall to wall. Even if she didn't feel confident, she could sound the part.

He flicked his flashlight up so that it illuminated his chin as though he was going to tell her a scary campfire story. "You got me." His eyebrows lifted and lowered in quick succession, as a twisted grin spread across his face.

She'd seen him around for years in the small town. He was a respected businessman, and the only one who seemed to be continually prosperous and upbeat in the face of the tire plant's layoffs. Apparently he had some extra income, and the twist in her stomach told her she already knew where it was coming from.

Forcing herself to take a step forward, she put her fists on her hips and pushed her shoulders back. "What do you want with me, Jimmy?"

His laugh, as he flashed the light back in her direction,

was cheerful and pleasant—which was somehow creepier than if he'd sounded completely sinister. "I think you know what you took of mine. I want it back."

"Her. You want *her* back. But you can't have her."

The corner of his mouth twisted again. "I think you'll change your mind soon enough. A couple nights in here, away from your precious house and those stupid girls, and you'll be ready to spill everything you know."

"I'm not telling you a thing."

"All right, then. If that's how you want to be, maybe you just want to take her place." He walked the few steps up to her, no longer blocking the light from the hall that spilled inside. She twitched as he brought one finger to her cheek, dragging it all the way to her chin. "I bet you're as pure as new snow. I could get a pretty penny for you."

The shudder that racked her whole body couldn't be contained at his vile words, and it made him smile. With a swipe of her arm, she pushed his hand away. "Don't touch me."

His reaction was instant. Her cheek lit on fire before she even heard the crack of his hand against her face, whipping her head to the side. "I'll do whatever I want. And I want to get my girl back. I have an eager buyer whose patience is running out. Understand?"

She glared at him, crossing her arms so she didn't give him the satisfaction of seeing her massage the imprint of his palm on her face. She'd learned that trick with Paul. Never let him see her pain.

He snickered as he turned his back on her. "Maybe that new boyfriend of yours will make a trade for you. How much does he really love you?"

"Don't—" The door swung shut behind him, cutting off her words, as she sank to the floor, no strength left in her legs to even make it to the mattress.

What was Matt going to do? He wouldn't trade Joy for her, would he?

Her stomach tossed like a ship on stormy seas.

He had to know that it was useless. Jimmy would never let her live once he got Joy back. She could identify him, and he had to know that she would turn him into the authorities the moment she was free.

Maybe Matt hadn't even returned to the house by now? Whenever "now" was. It could be thirty minutes since her kidnapping or three days. Did Matt even know she was missing?

Jimmy was counting on Matt's love for her, but what if there wasn't any?

She pressed a hand over her mouth, covering rapid breaths and battling sudden tears. What if he really didn't care for her? She'd practically begged him to kiss her the first time, and then they'd never talked about it.

Oh, there was tenderness in his touch, but always a distance in his eyes, as though he was holding something back. Until he'd told her about his childhood. He'd opened up to her about that, had even admitted that he was telling her things he'd never told anyone before. But was that love?

Did it even matter? Love couldn't unlock her handcuffs or put Jimmy in a prison cell of his own, where he belonged.

The sudden shortness in her chest answered that question in an instant.

It absolutely mattered. She cared if he cared about her, because her unnamed feelings for him were far outside the realm of just friendship.

Then again, maybe her emotions didn't matter.

If she didn't escape, Jimmy was going to kill her anyway.

* * *

Matt grabbed for the phone on Ashley's desk, speaking before it reached his ear. "Yes?"

"I want my property back." The voice on the other end stayed gruff, like the man was trying to disguise it.

I want mine back, too. "Where's Ashley?"

"First, I want that little Asian kid. And I want her now."

"She's not here."

"Fine. Then your precious little pain in my neck will take her place."

Matt's gut clenched, his head throbbing at the very idea of Ashley at the mercy of this lunatic. "I can bring her to you, but it'll take some time to get her back to town." With lives on the line—with *Ashley's* life on the line—it was amazingly easy to lie.

"How long?"

"At least forty-eight hours."

"Unacceptable. Make it no more than twenty-four."

He glanced at the clock on the wall beside Ashley's desk. That wasn't much time, but his team had designed and executed a rescue in less. It was almost five. She'd already been gone for more than eight hours and Tristan could only be two or three more hours away from Charity Way. "All right. Where do you want to make the swap?"

"There's an old warehouse at the corner of Lexington and Fourth. You know where that is?"

"Yes." He knew it well. He'd left two of this guy's men tied up there that morning.

"Eight tomorrow night. Come alone. No cops."

"No cops," Matt said. That didn't mean no SEALs. There would be at least five of them. And maybe the whole boat crew if Tristan had his way.

Of course, they wouldn't be at the meeting spot either. They'd find this guy's hiding hole long before that. And they definitely wouldn't be bringing along cops—cops wouldn't condone the methods Matt imagined they'd use to put the fear of SEAL into the traffickers. And as for the guy who'd kidnapped Ashley…by the time they were done, he'd be praying for the red-and-blue lights of a cruiser to appear.

The other man disconnected the call with no indication he'd noticed their conversation was missing an integral question, one that every hostage negotiator knew to ask. What was the hostage's condition? Was there proof Ashley was still alive?

Matt dropped his head into his hands, covering his whole face as he leaned on the desk top.

It was a question he just wasn't sure he wanted answered. Bad news would make it harder to concentrate, harder to think about anything but having her back in his arms. Good news might be even worse. How could he put together a plan while dreaming about what a future with her might look like? Would she ever leave Charity Way? Would he be willing to leave the teams to be with her?

Too many questions and no answers. There were no answers to any of them, including how she felt about him. Maybe she still thought of him as her brother's friend—a surrogate big brother.

A little voice in his ear told him that wasn't very likely given the way she'd kissed him. Twice.

But all of this was just a distraction from what he needed to focus on—the challenge of planning a rescue mission without intel or outside support.

The truth was he'd broken one of the cardinal rules of his SEAL training. He was emotionally involved with this mission. On a very real and far too personal level.

"Oh, Lord, let me focus right now. Protect Ashley and give me the strength to do this well."

His cell phone buzzed across the desk, and he scooped it up before it could fall off the edge. "Waterstone."

"Matt-o." Vince's tenor singsonged his name.

"Do you have a name for me?"

"For you? But of course." Vince clearly wanted to celebrate his discovery, but there wasn't time for it.

"Who?"

"Well, first I had to go through archived property records from twenty years ago to find out that—"

Matt scraped his fingers down his face, shoulders hunched against the instinct to yell at the civilian, who clearly didn't understand the situational urgency. "I get it. You're brilliant. Who is it?"

"James Swift ring any bells?"

"The guy who owns the local tire plant?"

"Yep."

He held out his right hand, glaring at it. He'd been two feet from the man and hadn't punched him. What he'd give to have that moment to live over again! And that cleared up another piece of the puzzle—Miranda's connection to Joy. Miranda worked for Swift. She must have found out what was going on, and figured out a way to smuggle Joy to Ashley.

"Are you impressed?"

Matt grinned. "I'd be more impressed if you could tell me exactly where he is right now."

"No can do. Sorry."

"Well, can you tell me if he owns any other property in the area?"

"He doesn't. But I can tell you that the tire plant has sure been under some…interesting construction in the last two years."

"What do you mean 'interesting'?"

Vince tapped away on his keyboard as he filled in the

details. "You ever know a tire plant to need underground storage?"

Ashley's phone burst to life. "Got to go. Thanks for the info." He picked up her office line again, a familiar pit growing in his stomach.

"This is Matt."

"Senior Chief. This is Chief Donal."

"Sir?" His words were clipped for the man who hadn't uncovered anything about the threat against Ashley and might even be aiding the culprit behind a human-trafficking ring—Matt hadn't forgotten that the chief and Swift were poker buddies. Matt had no time to waste on the head of the police force. He still had three buildings to check out before Tristan and the others arrived.

"Listen, son, Ashley called me this morning and asked me to look into a possible missing-person case. I've been trying to call her all day, but her phone is going straight to voice mail. She seemed spooked this morning, but now she's not responding. Do you know where she is?"

"What missing person did she ask you about?"

"An Asian girl. I'm pretty sure there's a report on her from out of San Francisco, so someone better tell me what's going on. Now."

Could the chief be trusted? Had he known about Swift's underground dealings? Or was he taken in by a seemingly up-front businessman, too?

"Someone's taken Ashley."

The chief gasped and spluttered, choking on a drink. "Who? What's going on?"

"The man who's after the missing girl. He wants to make a trade."

"Well, don't do it!" The chief's voice rose until he was yelling. "These things always end up with someone dead.

Whatever you do, don't take that girl to be traded. I assume you have a plan in place to get Ashley back."

He'd never heard the old guy so riled up, and he scaled down his defenses.

"I'm thinking on it."

"Well, don't think on it. Do something. How can I help?"

The battle inside his brain rivaled even those from the Great War. He couldn't very well give away his initial rescue plan to a man he didn't implicitly trust. But he could sure use an extra man in the field, especially one familiar with the area.

"I need to know where Ashley is being held before I can make any real plans."

"I can find that out." The chief stopped for a moment, the wheels in his brain probably working overtime as he realized the truth. "Actually…I don't even know where to start."

"I do. Can you check out both of these addresses? I just need to know if there's any activity going on there. Of any kind. But whatever you do, don't go in without backup. Stay a good distance away."

"What do you think is going on there?"

"If these guys will kidnap innocent girls, who knows what they're into?" He sidestepped the question, not eager to tell the chief something he might already know. If the chief was working with Swift, there was no use letting them know that someone was onto their business.

"Good point. Give me the addresses."

Matt read the chief the locations of the two buildings he hadn't yet checked, and the other man promised to call him as soon as he arrived at the first spot.

As soon as they hung up, Matt stood and paced the tiny office. It only took two steps to reach the opposite wall, but he continued back and forth, back and forth, as his muscles trembled in anticipation. His gut clenched twice, and he took corresponding deep breaths.

Ashley needed him, and he was coming for her. As long as he could find her.

He had a pretty good idea where to start looking.

He grabbed his black jacket, ducked his head into the living room and stared right at Lil. "I'm heading out. Don't leave the house for any reason. Don't answer the phone, and please don't let anyone else in."

The wrinkles on her lower lip quivered, but she gave a short nod. "When will you be back?"

"When I have Ashley."

He turned then, marching toward the front door and down the front steps, taking even breaths with every footfall. By the time he reached his truck, he was as cool as he'd ever been on a mission.

As he slammed his truck door, the phone in his pocket vibrated. "Waterstone."

"Sawyer."

Tristan sounded like he'd been raked across the coals. It was bad enough being in Charity Way and knowing the situation. Being miles away and not having a clue about the players must be killing him.

"I think I know where she is. I'm heading over there to recon right now."

"Who is it? Who has her?" His voice came out tight, like every word cost him a punch to the gut.

"It's a local business owner. I think he's using his factory as a warehouse for his trafficking."

"Where are we meeting him?"

"He thinks we're meeting at one of his other locations to swap the other girl for Ashley. But we're going to meet him tonight in his underground lair."

Tristan, who gave his laughs away like candy and always had a response, said nothing.

"How far out are you?"

"About ninety minutes. I'll call when we get there. By then, you'll know for sure where she is." It wasn't a question or a request. It was an order.

"I wi—" Tristan hung up before he could finish his promise.

Tristan had never been this mad in all the years they'd been friends. Tired, exhausted and grumpy? Sure. But he was downright furious at this point. So angry that he hadn't bothered to notice one thing.

Matt punched the steering wheel as he sailed toward the tire plant. When Tristan cooled off enough to realize that his best friend had fallen in love with Ashley, things were going to get even worse. If that was possible.

He parked his truck in a grove of trees half a mile from the plant and got out to hoof it the rest of the way. Anybody with that much to lose wouldn't let just anyone sneak up on him, and the truck was way too conspicuous.

As the sun disappeared completely, he pulled on his jacket to ward off the cool night breeze, moving silently from tree to tree for cover and forcing himself to wait at every third tree and listen.

Birds chirped and the leaves in the trees rustled against each other.

No other noise penetrated the night air, not even the sound of his steps as he approached the outer perimeter of the plant. The smell of melting rubber was thick in the air; he wrinkled his nose but pressed on.

Empty parking lots surrounded the building on three sides, and he followed the edge of the tree line to the back. Squatting there, he waited in the shadows.

After about five minutes, a man with a handgun walked through the beam of a floodlight. He took his time strolling by the back door, turning in slow circles but never looking into the woods. His eyes swept over the brown grass, though he never stopped long enough to actually see what he was looking at.

Amateur.

He had a big gun but zero know-how when it came to security.

When the guard disappeared, Matt checked for cameras sweeping the area. The only one was at the far corner of the building and easy enough to avoid, as it pointed into the parking lot.

Swift was counting on a lot here to leave the building where he kept his women relatively unprotected. Either that, or he assumed that no one would ever be coming after him.

He clearly thought he had the authorities in his pocket.

Maybe he did.

Maybe weekly poker games with the police chief and mayor and a good-old-boy attitude was all it took to fly under the radar in this small town.

Matt punched his leg. Had he made a grave mistake in asking Donal to look into those other buildings?

Maybe.

His phone shook against his leg.

Maybe not.

"Waterstone, this is Donal." The chief spoke before he could even greet him. "I went to both of those buildings. They're empty…but something is definitely going on there."

"What kind of something?" He'd play the fool as long as it took to know which side Donal was really on.

"I'm not sure exactly…but I have a feeling it's bad news. Like the kind of bad news that includes people being held against their will." The chief grunted when Matt didn't offer a response. "Like maybe someone's shuttling people through my town." His voice rose, probably right along with his blood pressure. "You know anything about this?"

"I guess about as much as you now."

The chief muttered something under his breath, and then was silent for several long seconds. "I'm going to call in an ICE team to check out these buildings."

Immigration and Customs Enforcement. He'd been so focused on getting Ashley back safely that he hadn't even thought about the jurisdiction. Of course, if there were illegal aliens being trafficked, someone from ICE had to be made aware.

"Where are you?" the chief asked.

"I'm looking into another lead."

"You're not going to give me an inch, are you, son?"

"Not even half of one, sir. Not when it comes to Ashley's safety."

"Fair enough." The chief sounded as though he'd have laughed if the call had been under any other set of circumstances. "I'll call into the closest ICE office and see how soon they can have a team out here."

If the chief was calling in ICE, he couldn't be involved with Swift. *Could he?*

Matt took a deep breath, deciding on the spot that he needed to trust the older man, who had been up front with him since the beginning.

"Think you could get them to meet me when they get to town?"

"Probably. You'll have to tell me where you are, you know."

He shrugged in the darkness. "I will. When they get here."

"I'll call you back." The chief hung up, leaving him to wait and watch.

Waiting wasn't his favorite part of recon. But ending up in a sticky spot that could have been avoided by learning the layout was worse.

The same security guard showed up ten minutes after his first appearance. Same easy amble, as though he had nowhere to be and nothing to protect.

Maybe he didn't even know what was hidden inside that building.

Matt waited ten minutes for the guard to appear and disappear for a third time before running to the building, pressing his back against it and checking for a tail when he got there.

The cold brick wall snagged his jacket, but he didn't stop sliding along it toward the gray metal door. By the raging beam of the floodlight, he jiggled the handle. The lock stuck in place, and he sighed. Of course it wouldn't be that easy.

He looked toward the full moon. He'd asked for a little bit of help. This would be a great time for it to arrive.

Just then, voices rose from the ground next to him.

"The boss said he's coming back tomorrow at six so we can move her."

"In the morning?"

Someone got slugged with the unmistakable sound of a fist buried into flesh. "Of course in the morning."

The ground just to his right rose, revealing a door to a cellar. His heart picked up speed, and he pressed his hands against his pant legs.

He'd done this a thousand times in practice and in the real world. So why were his palms sweating and pulse beating so loudly he was sure the two thugs would be able to hear him?

Ashley's face flashed across his mind's eye.

He'd never had so much at stake before.

SIXTEEN

Matt clenched his fists, remaining otherwise motionless as the two men climbed from the underground lair, calling down to one of their comrades that they'd return after a few hours of sleep in time to move the blonde.

That had to be Ashley.

The sod-covered door fell back into place, the noise cushioned by something clearly meant to keep the entrance a secret.

He took a quick breath before lunging at them, knocking both of them to their knees with quick strikes to the sides of their necks with the sharp sides of his hands. They groaned as they fell forward. In a second flat, he flipped them, giving each a solid punch to the solar plexus before hooking his arms through one of theirs and dragging them toward the tree line as they gasped for air.

"Nice move."

He dropped the men immediately, looking into the face of Will Gumble, one of the men on his boat crew.

"Willie G." He leaned forward and hugged the man who was as much annoying little brother as teammate. "How did you guys find me?"

Zach McCloud and Jordan Somerton, two other team members, looked up from where they knelt on the ground, pulling zip ties around the wrists of Swift's goons.

"Willie tracked the GPS on your cell phone."

Will, the team's communications and technology specialist, shrugged. "Thanks to the United States Navy, you're easier to find than a cornfield in Nebraska."

"Whose idea was it? I know you three didn't come up with it."

Zach pushed a thumb over his shoulder. "The L.T. suggested it."

Sure enough, Tristan stood about ten yards behind the others in the shadow of a pine tree. Feet shoulder-width apart, fists loose at his sides and face a mask of stone. He was ready for a fight. It didn't take much to figure out who would be on the other end of the brawl.

Matt stared at his oldest friend. "Glad you guys made it."

Tristan blinked but made no other indication that he'd heard what had been said.

Jordan, always the first to diffuse a tense situation, jumped in after he finished trussing one of the men on the ground. "Tell us what happened. From the start."

His stomach lurched.

From the start included two kisses, an untold number of stolen glances and a deep-seated longing for a future with Ashley that could never be.

One more glance at Tristan's flared nostrils and squinting eyes, and he knew it was a bad idea to share those details before they went into action. Not that there would ever be a right time.

The men huddled together like they were preparing for a play on the football field, and he filled them in on the notes and the threats, the smashed windshield and brick through the window. They laughed at him when he confessed to not catching the man in Ashley's yard his first day in town, and he swallowed his instinct to defend his mistake.

Nothing about this mission had gone like it was supposed to.

Especially his feelings for Ashley.

When he finally had them all up to speed, Zach said, "So what now?"

"Swift will be wherever Ashley is by oh six hundred. I think she's underground right now, but we can't afford to blow our surprise. We have to get Swift. If we go in to rescue her and tip him off, she'll never be safe." Bile rose from his stomach again, his lungs suddenly forgetting how to breathe. She was seventy-five yards away, and he could do nothing.

"So what's the plan?" Jordan's eyebrows raised in anticipation.

"Well, there are probably several girls inside—maybe as many as ten. At least that's the most the other building could hold. But I'm only sure about Ashley being in there. My best guess is that Swift tries to keep the women together, so he can concentrate all of his security on one location."

Will looked over at the building then back at Tristan. "So how do we know which one is Ashley?"

Tristan dug in the side pocket of his black cargo pants and pulled out his phone where a picture of Ashley and their mom filled the screen. The men passed it around quickly until Will whistled low. "Wow! L.T., you never told us your sister was such a babe."

"Shut it," Matt said.

Will smirked. "Aw, are you sweet on the L.T.'s sister, Senior Chief?"

Zach elbowed the kid in his side, but it didn't stop the low whistle that followed the verbal jab.

Tristan growled, "He wouldn't dare. He's known her since she was a kid."

Matt caught his best friend's eye, holding the gaze and trying to say what couldn't be said. "She's not a kid anymore."

Tristan squinted back, head cocked to the side and confusion filling every line on his face as he tugged his black cap over his ears. "You have something you want to say?" he finally asked.

This was neither the time nor the place to drop this bomb. Explosives were temperamental. They required careful planning and gentle hands. They needed to be planned for and prepared for.

This bomb took absolutely none of that into account.

But he couldn't keep it in a minute longer.

"I'm in love with Ashley."

Tristan's eyebrows furrowed, his usual smile a distant memory. "That's not funny."

Will laughed out loud and slapped at Zach's shoulder as he took in the scene with delight. Jordan clapped a hand on Tristan's arm. The giant of a man held the team's ranking officer back.

"I know. I didn't mean for it to happen." Matt blew out a slow breath but never looked away. "But she's an amazing woman."

"Did you…did you…"

He could see the wheels in Tristan's head spinning, trying to put the puzzle pieces together.

Tristan glared at him hard and shook off Jordan's hand, taking one step forward. He jammed a finger into Matt's chest, his words coming out through clenched teeth. "What did you do to her?"

"Nothing." He battled the urge to look away, to regain his composure in the face of his friend's fury. But that might be construed as regret or guilt. He had nothing to be ashamed of. "I would never treat her with anything less than respect. She's incredible. You know that. I know you do. You tell us all the time."

"He's right, L.T. You do say that a lot."

Tristan flashed a death glare at a suddenly silent Will before turning back to the source of his true anger. "So you love her so much you let her get kidnapped?"

The words stung like a gunshot.

Albeit, one he deserved.

Jordan stepped between them, hands up to both of their chests. "All right. Let's get our gear on and be ready. You can finish this after she's safe again."

"No need." Tristan spit out his words like the topic left a bad taste in his mouth. "We're done now. Just like whatever little romance Waterstone's had going with my baby sister. It's over. *Now.* He was my best friend, but no one's good enough for Ashley. Not after everything she's been through."

It was true. He wasn't good enough for her.

His phone lit up again with another call from Donal. "What do you have?"

"There's an ICE team on their way to town. And if the missing girl is the one in the system, her family recently immigrated. ICE has the jurisdiction here. But maybe they'll take your help on this one."

"Thanks, Chief. We're in the grove of trees on the backside of the tire plant."

"The tire plant?" Donal's voice dropped, his words pained. "Please tell me Jimmy isn't involved in this. He wouldn't do this. He's been a guest in my home. We've played cards for years." His voice rose with every sentence.

Matt genuinely wished he didn't have to be the one to

break it to the man, but he wouldn't lie now either. "I'm sorry."

Donal's heavy sigh was the only response, but Matt didn't have time to console him. "We'll wait for the ICE team, and then we're going in to get Ashley back."

Ashley grabbed at her stomach, as if she could physically push away the hunger pangs. She hadn't eaten in hours, or possibly days. There was no telling the passing of time within the secluded cement walls. But her stomach still growled to be fed, demanding attention and receiving only the laughter of the guards pacing outside the cell door.

She curled into a ball on the mattress, praying for sleep or anything else to take her mind off this place, but a suitable distraction refused to come.

Out of habit she pulled on the metal cuff, which only chafed against her bone, tearing at the skin that had rubbed raw. She flinched away as if it was scalding water, fire billowing up her arm.

It wasn't supposed to be like this. She was supposed to be able to get free. She was stronger than this.

Except she wasn't.

She was completely helpless and at the mercy of men who'd rather laugh at her than help her.

"Oh, God." Tears streamed out of the corners of her eyes as she stared at the blocks of the ceiling, imagining a cloudless blue sky beyond it. She tucked folded hands beneath her chin, taking a stuttered breath. "I'm not strong enough to make it through this alone. I don't want to do this without Matt, and I know I can't survive it without You. I'm weak, and I need You to be strong for me right now."

The click of a key in the lock of her door had her on her feet in an instant, fists ready at her sides. When the door opened, the light was blinding, but she didn't step back from it.

"You ready for a little trip?" Jimmy asked. "It's time to get ready for a trade."

"No. Matt won't do it. And I won't let him. Take me instead—just leave Joy alone."

His laughter made her skin crawl. "Oh, I will."

She blinked rapidly, her eyes finally adjusting to the light. "What's that mean?"

"You stupid girl." He walked up to her, running a knuckle along her jawline, and she jerked away. "You pretend to help those women, but you have no idea what they're going through. You will soon, though."

She bit her bottom lip to keep it from shaking. "You're not getting her back."

"Oh, I will get her back. And I'm going to keep you to repay me for all the trouble you've caused."

"But people will be looking for me. I'll be missed."

He motioned to the giant standing at the door, pointing to her hand. "Good thing I have connections with the right people. Do you think my poker buddies would seriously look at me as a suspect in the disappearance of a woman known to stick her nose where it doesn't belong?"

Jimmy's henchman unlocked her shackle, and she couldn't help but massage the painful sores there. But she didn't have much time before his enormous hands yanked her arms behind her back and zipped her hands together with plastic ties that cut into the lesions already there.

She bit down on her tongue, squeezing her eyes against the searing pain and forcing herself not to cry out.

Jimmy sneered, obviously enjoying her discomfort. "Let's go." He grabbed her arm, leaving finger marks around her biceps as he dragged her into the hallway lined with four identical doors on each side of the walkway.

The goon who had tied her up had to duck his head so he didn't run into one of the mesh-covered lightbulbs as he led them toward a bend in the hallway.

Movement wasn't good. As long as she stayed in one place, Matt might be able to find her. But if Jimmy moved her around, she might never be found. She might end up like he said.

The thought made her stomach lurch, and she yanked her arm, trying to break Jimmy's hold. He only laughed and squeezed tighter.

"Oh, come on. You'll have to try harder than that."

Panic narrowed her line of sight, and she gulped air like it would run out. She kicked at his knee, managing to elicit a grunt when she connected with his shin.

"You'll pay for that." He lifted the back of his hand, and she recoiled, already knowing the sting of that motion.

Just before his knuckles connected with her cheek, something popped and sparks exploded from the lightbulb in front of them.

Several women screamed behind their doors, and Jimmy let loose a string of obscenities before demanding to know what had happened. "Go check on that." He shoved his man into the dimness of the hall's corner.

A fragile piece of hope bloomed in her chest like a flower wishing for spring.

Had Matt found her?

Suddenly the wall moved, and Jimmy's thug fell to the floor.

But it wasn't the wall that had dropped the giant. There was someone there.

Now hope surged in her chest, growing stronger every moment, and she pulled on her arm, trying to break free of Jimmy's grip.

Jimmy swung her in front of him. Reaching into his

pocket, he pulled out something she couldn't see. When he pressed the freezing metal against her neck, she didn't have to guess that it was a gun.

"Who are you? What do you want?"

Two shadows materialized from the darkness into the feeble light, both dressed in all black from the beanies on their heads to the paint on their faces to the boots on their feet. Even the pistols in their hands blended into their midnight camouflage.

Two more figures appeared behind them, more visible in navy blue jackets with the letters I.C.E. over their hearts.

She didn't have to see his face to know that Matt stood before her, his shoulders stretching the cotton of his long-sleeve shirt. A flak vest added bulk to his usually trim midsection, but his eyes were unmistakable.

He stared at her, as though asking for something he couldn't verbalize.

She wanted to smile, to reassure him that she was all right. That the gun at her neck didn't scare her, but she couldn't do any more than bite her lips against the tightness in her throat.

Jimmy swore violently, but all she could hear was the beating of her heart, which slowed with each subtle nod of Matt's chin. His eyes slowly looked left, and she followed his line of sight.

Tristan stood just behind Matt, his handgun also raised and eyes trained on Jimmy.

"Let her go, Swift." Matt's tone brooked no argument, but Jimmy wasn't smart enough to hear it.

"Seems like you're in no position to be making orders."

"This can't end well for you. Let her go, now." The low timbre of his voice made her toes curl. How had she ever worried that he wouldn't come for her?

"It's not going to happen. Let us out of here, or I shoot

her. Now." His hand shook the gun at her neck, and she took another steadying breath just to stay on her feet, her knees threatening to give out.

Matt stared hard into her eyes, the blue in his own cutting through the wan light. "I've seen this kind of thing end badly. Like three bullets to the chest badly. It's not going to be good for you, Swift. Do you understand?"

Her eyes flew open. He wasn't talking to Jimmy at all. He was talking to her. He was asking if she understood. What? What was she supposed to understand?

And then the memory flooded in. The mission where the woman fainted. They'd shot the terrorist three times in the chest.

He wanted her to faint. Or at least fall to the ground.

He wanted her completely weak.

He wanted her to trust that he could be there to save her.

"Do you understand?" He blinked once, very slowly.

Jimmy said something that was drowned out by blood rushing through every vein in her body; her extremities tingled as she blinked a perfect echo to his.

He lifted the corner of his mouth, and she closed her eyes, letting her entire body relax. For a moment she was floating, and then she crashed to the floor, falling hard on her shoulder and crying out as four bullets blew over her head and plowed Jimmy to the ground.

When she looked up a split second later, she expected to see Matt over her, but instead it was Tristan who scooped her up. His embrace nearly stole her breath as he carried her past several other men in black and up a set of stairs.

Over his shoulder she glimpsed Matt kicking Jimmy's gun away and hovering over his body. He didn't even look in her direction.

SEVENTEEN

Three weeks later

Matt snapped yet another pen tip against the report he was supposed to be writing. Ink leaked onto the sheet of paper, and he crumpled the paper into a ball, tossing it into the trash can next to his desk before pulling out the third blank report in twenty minutes.

He'd never get the thing written at this rate.

A sharp rap on the door drew his attention to Willie G., who leaned a shoulder against the door frame. He'd changed out of his BDUs, clearly looking forward to their weekend off.

"You coming with us, Senior? Some of us are going to play a game of pool."

He tapped a fresh pen against his blank report, wishing that something—anything—would take his mind off the only thing he'd been able to think about since returning to active duty. He'd run every physical drill on autopilot and passed every test the medical staff at the infirmary had thrown at him.

His body was back to normal, but his mind was five hundred miles away from the base at Coronado.

Stuck at a yellow house in Charity Way.

"Not today, Will. You guys go have a good time." He looked back at the page on his desk, then back up to add, "Don't do anything stupid."

"Oh, come on, Senior. You haven't been out with us once since you got back from leave."

The skin across his shoulders felt too tight, the nerves in his legs suddenly bouncing. He'd been like this far too long. But there wasn't a thing he could do about it.

Tristan had kept his promise. He stayed beside Ashley for hours as the cleanup crew from ICE and the local police had stormed the jail under the tire plant, freeing four other girls, including Miranda, whose story filled in all the gaps they'd needed.

She'd had a suspicion about Swift's underground activities, but when she found the proof she needed to turn him in, he threatened her daughter—the most important person in Miranda's life.

Joy had been a fluke. She'd fought her guards and run into the parking lot one night, where Miranda had seen her. Miranda had known that she couldn't take the girl to the police or Swift might follow through on his threat. Ashley had been her only hope to save Joy. Miranda just hadn't realized the lengths to which Swift would go to get her back for the high-paying buyer who had chosen Joy from her picture, and who wouldn't accept any substitutes.

From a distance, Matt had watched Ashley holding her friend, both women crying, both finally free.

He'd have done anything to join them, to wrap his arms around Ashley and hold on to her until she knew she never had to be afraid again. But he couldn't make promises like that.

Tristan had made sure of that.

And for good reason. Matt had nothing to offer her. He couldn't give her the life she deserved. His world was unstable and often chaotic—which suited him and suited the past that had made him into the man he was today. Hers was lists and cubbyholes. Simple and sweet—and way too ordered for him.

That's why Tristan had been so upset. He'd known that Matt wasn't the right fit.

But it didn't matter how many times he reminded himself of that. His heart still longed for her like no one else he'd ever met.

"Senior?" Will waved his outstretched hand. "You okay?"

No.

"Yes. I'm fine. Just have to finish this report. You boys have a good time. Don't do anything stupid."

Will smirked. "You already said that."

"It bears repeating for you guys."

Will disappeared down the hallway, leaving him alone with his report and the images of Ashley that just would not leave his mind. The way she looked lying on the couch after being shot at. The determination in her face when she insisted on going first into the Infinity. The peace in her eyes after he kissed her the first time.

How long would the images last?

Unfortunately he already knew the answer.

At another knock on his door, he bit down on the end of his pen without looking up. "I said I don't want to go." His voice felt more like a growl than Will deserved, so he swallowed and finished in a more agreeable tone. "Have fun without me."

"Truth is, I'm not having any fun without you."

He shot out of his chair like a grenade had exploded beneath it.

"Ashley." The word came out on a breath, and he cleared his throat, taking in every inch of her from her soft, blond hair to the pink toenails peeking through the tips of her shoes. "What are you doing here?"

She tugged the matching pink sweater closed under her chin, then forced her hands back to her sides, her gaze resting somewhere over his shoulder. He couldn't bother to look at what held her attention as he drank in the sweet sight of her.

She bit her lips until they vanished and blinked a few times. Her shoulders rose and fell with deep breaths. Finally she wrinkled her nose and smiled. "I came to see you."

He tried to put his hands in the pockets of his pants, but he'd suddenly forgotten how to use his arms.

There were no words to respond to her. Every thought that ran through his mind was just as inadequate as he was for her.

I've missed you.

I'm a wreck without you.

I want to hold you.

I'm so sorry I wasn't there for you when you needed me.

Say the word, and I'll move to Charity Way for you today.

I need you more than I need to be on the teams.

So he tried to change the subject. "How's Joy?"

Her teeth flashed under the fluorescent light. "She's wonderful. She's back with her family, who were looking for her." She stepped into the tiny office, two steps cutting the distance between them in half, and his breath caught in his chest. "Chief Donal brought them to Lil's for the reunion." Her cheeks flushed as she dropped her gaze. "I've never cried so hard in my life."

He gulped down the real questions he wanted to ask, offering instead, "Did the ICE agents find the man who was putting pressure on Swift?"

"Not yet. But Jimmy spilled everything about his operation and contacts hoping for a deal."

His fists clenched as he crossed his arms, one of his eyelids twitching. Swift deserved so much more than the plastic bullets that had taken him down but not seriously injured him. But the ICE agents had been clear that they needed his contacts. And if they could use him to take down a larger network of human traffickers, it was worth it to go easy.

Hopefully the court system wouldn't be as kind.

Another step brought her to the edge of the rickety metal desk. The smell of citrus shampoo and fresh laundry floated toward him, making him light-headed.

"Why are you here, Ashley?"

He'd never been so thankful for a piece of furniture in his life. Without the desk, he would certainly have scooped her into his arms and kissed her soundly. But she slipped even closer, pressing her hands to the desk as she leaned toward him. Couldn't she tell that he was seconds away from pushing the thing out of his way and pressing his lips to hers anyway?

Ashley took a deep breath, and prayed for the strength to say what she had to say. After all, if she wasn't honest with him, she'd always regret it.

"I came to see you."

"You said that already."

She held up her hand to ward off further interruptions. "I meant it. I had to tell you something."

But the words were gone.

This was so much harder than she'd imagined it would be. She'd practiced the speech—how she was going to tell him exactly what was on her mind. Except standing in the same room with him, her only thoughts revolved around having those arms, which were filling out his brown T-shirt quite nicely, holding her close.

"Do you remember when that brick hit me in the head and you tore off your sleeve to stop the bleeding?" His features like stone, he nodded. "No one has ever done anything like that for me."

"It wasn't a big deal."

"It was the first of many big deals."

Now it was his turn to hold up his hand to stop her speech. "Please, don't. Ashley, we both know that you deserve better. Better than a guy with no past and an uncertain future."

"Is that honestly who you think you are?"

He shook his head and stared at the ceiling while letting out a slow sigh. "You're doing amazing work in Charity Way, Ashley. But it's organized and ordered. I don't know what continent I'll be on from one day to the next or how long I'll even get to be a SEAL." He threw up his hands. "I don't even know my parents' names."

"I don't care."

"But you will. And I won't be the reason for your unhappiness." He still couldn't meet her gaze, so she skirted the desk and grabbed his wrists until he looked into her eyes.

Butterflies swarmed like the first time he'd kissed her—and the second.

With any luck there would be a third time.

"Matt, I've been scared for a really long time. What Paul did to me made me not just afraid of falling in love again, it made me afraid of life. I was scared that I wasn't enough to help other women. I was scared that I was too weak to help myself, let alone anyone else. So I put on this facade of strength. I wore courage like a coat, trying to convince everyone—including myself—that I could handle anything that came my way."

Her lower lip quivered, but she never looked away from the storm brewing in his eyes. "And then you came along. And you told me I didn't have to be strong all the time. You reminded me what it felt like to really rely on someone else. To let down my guard long enough to remember that when I'm weak, God is strong. And sometimes when we really need help, He sends navy SEALs to the rescue."

His eyebrows drew together. "You are one of the strongest women I've ever met. And if I hadn't left you alone, you'd never have needed to be rescued."

"Is that what this is about? Do you really think that my getting kidnapped is your fault?" She shook her head slowly. "That is entirely my fault. I knew I shouldn't go anywhere without you. I knew you'd come back. But I told myself I had to be strong without you. I didn't realize how much better I am with you."

He reached out a hand, sliding his fingers along her cheekbone until his palm cupped her face. "I'd always come back for you."

Her knees shook, and she grabbed at his arm to stabilize herself. "I know. I was being so stupid."

He took two small steps in her direction, a muscle in his jaw jumping with each movement. She mirrored each of his strides, slipping closer and closer to the wall. If she didn't have something to lean on soon, she'd crumble into a heap of nerves.

Or simply fall into his arms and never want to leave.

"Matt, you're the first person who's ever let me be strong enough to admit my own weaknesses." She bumped into the wall at her back and pressed her hands flat against the smooth surface as he rested his palms on either side of her head, holding her inside the confines of his arms.

What could have reminded her of a terrifying night in a cell instead wrapped around her like the warmth of a blanket on a chilly night.

"I think you're pretty incredible, Ashley Sawyer."

"You, too." She slipped her hands around his waist, the softness of his T-shirt contrasting with the solid wall of muscle it covered.

He leaned forward in a slow push-up, and her heart swelled, her eyes only on the gentle curve of his lips. But he stopped several inches short, pain sweeping across his face.

"Is your leg bothering you?"

"My leg?" He dipped his chin to stare at their toe-to-toe feet, his forehead brushing hers before looking back up to meet her gaze. "No. I'm cleared for duty." The lines on either side of his mouth deepened. "But I'll retire so I can be with you in Charity Way."

"Don't be ridiculous. I'd never ask you to retire from the teams. It's too much a part of you. I've already worked it out with Lil that Carmen will take over as the director of the house for the time being. I'll find a place here to get involved—"

"I love you." He cemented his words by pressing his lips to hers as he wrapped his arms around her, holding her so close that she lost her breath. But breathing seemed a second-class necessity at the moment.

After several long seconds, he pulled back, and she gasped for the air her lungs had been deprived of.

When she could manage words again, she said, "I love you, too. I told Tristan—"

"Tristan." He cut her off again, this time much less pleasantly. "He's going to hate this."

"He'll learn to live with it." She pressed a hand over his racing heart. It was speeding like that because of her. Of course, hers was doing the same because of him. "I told him he was going to have to get over his objections because I'm not getting over you."

A slow smile spread across his face, and she pressed up to her tiptoes to kiss his smooth-shaven cheek. "He just wants someone who will take care of me. And no one can do that like you. I told him you've been part of our family for years, and that's not going to change. Ever."

His smile grew with each passing second until he shook his head and pulled her in for another toe-curling kiss.

"I could get used to this," he whispered against her mouth.

"You better."

EPILOGUE

Eight months later

"Miss Ashley is waiting for you, Mr. Tristan."

Matt glanced over his shoulder at the young boy who peeked around the door frame.

"I'll be right there, Julio." Tristan clapped a hand on Matt's shoulder. "Are you ready for this?"

Matt swallowed, despite his dry mouth, and searched for any sign of hesitancy in his best friend's eyes. "I am. Are you?"

Tristan glanced at his feet and the brown dress shoes Matt had seen him wear only one other time in their entire friendship. When his gaze rose, his eyes were as blue as his sister's. "I didn't think anyone could ever be good enough for Ash." He stuck his hands into the pockets of his tan dress pants as a grin tugged across his face. "And you're not. But watching you two together is like seeing two pieces of a puzzle that fit just right."

Thumping his friend on the back, Matt matched his grin. "She is pretty amazing. Sometimes I still can't believe she fell in love with me."

"That makes two of us." Tristan's laughter filled the groom's dressing room at the beachside resort. As Matt adjusted his tie for the last time and straightened the cuffs of his white shirt, Tristan turned serious. "I know it took me a little while to come around about you guys being together, but there's no one else in the world I'd rather see her marry. You're my brother and the best man I know. I don't have to tell you to take care of her, because I know you will."

His words still lingering in the room, Tristan disappeared, heading for the bride's room, where he'd meet Ashley and walk her down the aisle.

Tristan was right. Matt didn't need to be reminded to take care of her.

He'd put his life on the line to protect Ashley. And by the grace of God, he'd never again get as close to losing her as he had the year before.

As he walked onto the beach, passing rows of white folding chairs filled with their friends and family, he smiled. In just a few minutes he'd be joined by his bride.

When he reached his pastor on the open beach, they shook hands. "You're looking pretty pleased with yourself right about now," Pastor Rick said.

"Am I?" He didn't bother trying to lose his smile. "Well, you know Ashley. I've got good reason to be happy right now."

Rick laughed just as the string quartet began their tune. On the boardwalk by the resort, little Greta appeared, leaving a wake of white flower petals as she sashayed down the red aisle. When she reached him, she looked all the way up and whispered, "She looks just like a princess."

His heart twisted at that moment, and his breath caught somewhere in his chest. There she was, a vision in white walking toward him and looking as if she was holding on to Tristan's arm for all she was worth.

When she stood before him, he held out his hand and

she grabbed it with trembling fingers. For her ears only, he said, "Don't worry. I've got you."

The light in her eyes and the joy in her smile released the tension in his chest as Rick started the ceremony. And then he was repeating the words he'd practiced, promising to love and honor and cherish her always. Promising her a future filled with his love. Because that's all he could give her.

He couldn't change his past. But the truth was that his childhood didn't matter anymore. He wasn't the men who had raised him, and the statistics didn't define him. Because where he was uncertain, God was sure. Where he was weak, God was strong.

"You may now kiss your bride."

Matt didn't need to be told twice, pulling her into his embrace and beginning to make good on the promises he'd just spoken.

* * * * *

Dear Reader,

Thank you for joining Ashley and Matt on this adventure. I hope their story has encouraged you to embrace and boast in your own weaknesses, so that Christ's strength can rest on you. Take heart, friends, for we serve a good God, capable of mighty things. I hope you've been reminded of that through this story.

I knew from the start that this story would feature Matt, a United States Navy SEAL, and Ashley, the sister of a SEAL, but human trafficking wasn't always a part of their tale. As I began reading about the plight of women and children caught in slavery and trafficking, my heart broke for them, just as I knew Matt's and Ashley's would. I think caring for victims of human trafficking falls under Jesus' instruction to care for "the least of these." If you'd like to learn more about human trafficking and how to take a stand against it, I encourage you to visit www.ijm.org, home of the International Justice Mission.

I hope you've enjoyed Matt and Ashley's book. I'd love to connect with you through my website:

www.lizjohnsonbooks.com

Twitter:

@lizjohnsonbooks

Email:

liz@lizjohnsonbooks.com

Or Facebook:

www.facebook.com/lizjohnsonbooks.

May you rest in God's strength every day,

Liz Johnson

Questions for Discussion

1. What was your favorite part of the book or your favorite character? Why?

2. From the beginning of the book, we see that Ashley has a very close relationship with her brother. Do you have a brother? Are you as close as Ashley and Tristan?

3. How do you think their father's death when they were younger affected Ashley and Tristan?

4. Matt had a very different childhood than the Sawyers. How would you compare your own early years to theirs?

5. Ashley's family accepted Matt as one of their own because he was Tristan's best friend. Have you ever welcomed someone into your family like that? How did that affect you?

6. Matt and Ashley both carried secrets that motivated them to care for others. Have you ever had a secret like that? How did you deal with it?

7. When the time was right, Matt and Ashley shared their secrets with each other. Why do you think they knew it was safe to tell one another?

8. How do you decide when it's safe to tell a friend your secrets?

9. In daily life we may never deal with a man as duplicitous as Jimmy Swift, but we will likely meet people who say one thing and do another. Have you ever dealt with that? How did you handle the situation?

10. Do you think Tristan handled it well when he found out that Matt was in love with Ashley? How would you have responded in his place?

11. Toward the end, Ashley had to accept her own weakness and allow God to be strong when she couldn't be. Have you ever had to come to terms with this in your own life? How have you dealt with it?

12. Would you have left Lil's Place to move closer to Matt if you were in Ashley's shoes at the end of the book?

COMING NEXT MONTH
from Love Inspired® Suspense
AVAILABLE JANUARY 2, 2013

TRACKING JUSTICE
Texas K-9 Unit
Shirlee McCoy

Police detective Austin Black assures Eva Billows he'll find her son. With his search and rescue bloodhound Justice, Austin and Eva search all of Sagebrush, Texas. Eva trusts no one, but Austin—and Justice—won't disappoint her.

THE GENERAL'S SECRETARY
Military Investigations
Debby Giusti

The dying words of the man imprisoned for killing Lillie Beaumont's mother suggest hidden secrets. Special Agent Dawson Timmons agrees. Together, they face painful secrets, but Dawson fears that a murderer is waiting to strike again....

NARROW ESCAPE
Camy Tang

Arissa Tiong and her niece are kidnapped by a notorious drug gang, but Arissa escapes and runs to former narcotics cop Nathan Fischer. He's all that stands between her and the dangerous thugs who are after her.

MIDNIGHT SHADOWS
Carol Post

Escaping a stalker, Melissa Langston flees to her hometown. Only her ex-fiancé, Chris Jamison, a former cop, believes she's still in danger. The more Melissa turns to Chris, the more her stalker wants him gone—permanently.

Look for these and other Love Inspired books wherever books are sold, including most bookstores, supermarkets, discount stores and drugstores.

LISCNM1212

REQUEST YOUR FREE BOOKS!

2 FREE RIVETING INSPIRATIONAL NOVELS
PLUS 2 FREE MYSTERY GIFTS

YES! Please send me 2 FREE Love Inspired® Suspense novels and my 2 FREE mystery gifts (gifts are worth about $10). After receiving them, if I don't wish to receive any more books, I can return the shipping statement marked "cancel". If I don't cancel, I will receive 4 brand-new novels every month and be billed just $4.49 per book in the U.S. or $4.99 per book in Canada. That's a saving of at least 22% off the cover price. It's quite a bargain! Shipping and handling is just 50¢ per book in the U.S. and 75¢ per book in Canada.* I understand that accepting the 2 free books and gifts places me under no obligation to buy anything. I can always return a shipment and cancel at any time. Even if I never buy another book, the two free books and gifts are mine to keep forever.

123/323 IDN FEHR

Name _____ (PLEASE PRINT)

Address _____ Apt. #

City _____ State/Prov. _____ Zip/Postal Code

Signature (if under 18, a parent or guardian must sign)

Mail to the **Reader Service:**
IN U.S.A.: P.O. Box 1867, Buffalo, NY 14240-1867
IN CANADA: P.O. Box 609, Fort Erie, Ontario L2A 5X3

Not valid for current subscribers to Love Inspired Suspense books.

**Are you a subscriber to Love Inspired Suspense
and want to receive the larger-print edition?
Call 1-800-873-8635 or visit www.ReaderService.com.**

* Terms and prices subject to change without notice. Prices do not include applicable taxes. Sales tax applicable in N.Y. Canadian residents will be charged applicable taxes. Offer not valid in Quebec. This offer is limited to one order per household. All orders subject to credit approval. Credit or debit balances in a customer's account(s) may be offset by any other outstanding balance owed by or to the customer. Please allow 4 to 6 weeks for delivery. Offer available while quantities last.

Your Privacy—The Reader Service is committed to protecting your privacy. Our Privacy Policy is available online at www.ReaderService.com or upon request from the Reader Service.

We make a portion of our mailing list available to reputable third parties that offer products we believe may interest you. If you prefer that we not exchange your name with third parties, or if you wish to clarify or modify your communication preferences, please visit us at www.ReaderService.com/consumerschoice or write to us at Reader Service Preference Service, P.O. Box 9062, Buffalo, NY 14269. Include your complete name and address.

Love Inspired® SUSPENSE

RIVETING INSPIRATIONAL ROMANCE

TEXAS K-9 UNIT

Lawmen that solve the toughest cases with the help of their brave canine partners.

Follow Lone Star State police officers and their canine partners in action each month as they get closer to not only uncovering a mastermind criminal but also finding love.

TRACKING JUSTICE by **Shirlee McCoy**
January 2013

DETECTION MISSION by **Margaret Daley**
February 2013

GUARD DUTY by **Sharon Dunn**
March 2013

EXPLOSIVE SECRETS by **Valerie Hansen**
April 2013

SCENT OF DANGER by **Terri Reed**
May 2013

LONE STAR PROTECTOR by **Lenora Worth**
June 2013

Available wherever books are sold.

www.LoveInspiredBooks.com

LISCONT13R